Always and Forever, Cat.

The irony of that phrase haunted Rory Sullivan. Just because you left a place or a person didn't mean they left you. Some memories were burned too deep to ever depart; they remained in your mind, constant reminders of what was.

What was, what is, what would always be for him—the woman whose memory he'd tried to ignore. A woman he'd tried to erase from the deepest recesses of his mind but had found was unforgettable. The passion he tried so hard to bury was ultimately unquenchable.

Caitlyn Kildare was still there. In his heart. In his mind. In his past.

Was there someone special in her life now? Someone who'd replaced him in her heart, her mind…her bed?

Dear Reader,

Happy anniversary! Twenty years ago, in May, 1980, we launched Silhouette Books. Much has changed since then, but our gratitude to you, our many readers, and our dedication to bringing you the best that romance fiction has to offer, remains as true today as it did in 1980. Thank you for sharing with us the joy of romance, and for looking toward a wonderful future with us. The best is yet to come!

Those winsome mavericks are back with brand-new stories to tell beneath the Big Sky! *The Kincaid Bride* by Jackie Merritt marks the launch of the MONTANA MAVERICKS: WED IN WHITEHORN series, which focuses on a new generation of Kincaids. This heartwarming marriage-of-convenience tale leads into Silhouette's exciting twelve-book continuity.

Romance is in the air in *The Millionaire She Married,* a continuation of the popular CONVENIENTLY YOURS miniseries by reader favorite Christine Rimmer. And searing passion unites a fierce Native American hero with his stunning soul mate in *Warrior's Embrace* by Peggy Webb.

If you enjoy romantic odysseys, journey to exotic El Bahar in *The Sheik's Arranged Marriage* by Susan Mallery—book two in the sizzling DESERT ROGUES miniseries.

Gail Link pulls heartstrings with her tender tale about a secret child who brings two lovebirds together in *Sullivan's Child.* And to cap off the month, you'll adore *Wild Mustang* by Jane Toombs—a riveting story about a raven-haired horse wrangler who sweeps a breathtaking beauty off her feet.

It's a spectacular month of reading in Special Edition. Enjoy!

All the best,

Karen Taylor Richman
Senior Editor

Please address questions and book requests to:
Silhouette Reader Service
U.S.: 3010 Walden Ave., P.O. Box 1325, Buffalo, NY 14269
Canadian: P.O. Box 609, Fort Erie, Ont. L2A 5X3

GAIL LINK
SULLIVAN'S CHILD

Silhouette®

SPECIAL ▼ EDITION®

Published by Silhouette Books
America's Publisher of Contemporary Romance

To the two Jennifers (Nauss and Walsh) at Silhouette—
thanks for sharing in the creative process
and caring about my work.
To the terrific crew of Barnes & Noble Wilmington—
co-workers extraordinaire!
To Pierce Brosnan—from "Remington" to "Bond,"
you always deliver the goods.
It's a pleasure (not to mention an inspiration)
to watch you work.

SILHOUETTE BOOKS

ISBN 0-373-24325-1

SULLIVAN'S CHILD

Copyright © 2000 by Gail Link

This edition published by arrangement with Harlequin Books S.A.

® and TM are trademarks of Harlequin Books S.A., used under license.
Trademarks indicated with ® are registered in the United States Patent
and Trademark Office, the Canadian Trade Marks Office and in other
countries.

Visit Silhouette at www.eHarlequin.com

Printed in U.S.A.

Books by Gail Link

Silhouette Special Edition

Marriage To Be? #1035
Lone Star Lover #1121
Texan's Bride #1163
Sullivan's Child #1325

GAIL LINK

A bookseller since 1977, Gail realized her dream of becoming a published author with the release of her first novel, a historical, in 1989.

Gail is a member of the national Romance Writers of America and Novelists, Inc. She has been featured speaker at many writers' conferences, and several publications have featured her comments on the romance genre, including *Publishers Weekly* and the RWA Report. In 1993 Gail was nominated for *Romantic Times Magazine's* Reviewer's Choice Award for Best Sensual Historical.

In addition to being a voracious reader, Gail is also an avid musical theater and movie fan. She would love to hear from her readers, and you may write to her at P.O. Box 717, Concordville, PA 19331.

IT'S OUR 20th ANNIVERSARY!
We'll be celebrating all year,
Continuing with these fabulous titles,
On sale in May 2000.

Romance

 #1444 Mercenary's Woman
Diana Palmer

#1445 Too Hard To Handle
Rita Rainville

 #1446 A Royal Mission
Elizabeth August

#1447 Tall, Strong & Cool Under Fire
Marie Ferrarella

 #1448 Hannah Gets a Husband
Julianna Morris

#1449 Her Sister's Child
Lilian Darcy

Desire

 #1291 Dr. Irresistible
Elizabeth Bevarly

 #1292 Expecting His Child
Leanne Banks

#1293 In His Loving Arms
Cindy Gerard

 #1294 Sheikh's Honor
Alexandra Sellers

 #1295 The Baby Bonus
Metsy Hingle

#1296 Did You Say Married?!
Kathie DeNosky

Intimate Moments

 #1003 Rogue's Reform
Marilyn Pappano

 #1004 The Cowboy's Hidden Agenda
Kathleen Creighton

#1005 In a Heartbeat
Carla Cassidy

 #1006 Anything for Her Marriage
Karen Templeton

#1007 Every Little Thing
Linda Winstead Jones

 #1008 Remember the Night
Linda Castillo

Special Edition

#1321 The Kincaid Bride
Jackie Merritt

 #1322 The Millionaire She Married
Christine Rimmer

#1323 Warrior's Embrace
Peggy Webb

 #1324 The Sheik's Arranged Marriage
Susan Mallery

#1325 Sullivan's Child
Gail Link

#1326 Wild Mustang
Jane Toombs

Chapter One

"Mommy, what's a bastard?"

Coming right after the softly spoken question from her daughter, the sharp sound of the empty, oversize coffee mug that slipped from her fingers and crashed to the floor was almost inaudible to Caitlyn Kildare.

A soft gasp of breath caught in her throat.

What couldn't be heard in the sunny kitchen was the shattering of her world into even smaller fragments than that of the broken piece of crockery.

"Where did you hear that word?" Hadn't she known that this might happen someday? She'd told herself that she should be prepared, but being prepared and facing the reality were two very different things.

Getting a grip on her stunned emotions, Caitlyn turned around and faced the curious glance of her six-year-old daughter.

The little girl's eyes were wide. She stared at the mess

her mother had made on the floor, her dark blue eyes
outlined by a fringe of sooty lashes. Everything, including her stubborn chin, was a softer replica of her father.

Rory's daughter. A child he knew nothing about.

Cat bent down, picked up the pieces of the broken
mug, a souvenir of a touring Broadway show, and threw
them into the trash can.

Placing Tara in one of the sturdy maple chairs that
flanked the kitchen table, Cat hunkered down on her
knees before the child, gently stroking the soft, wavy,
long black hair. A sprinkle of fine golden freckles dusted
her daughter's nose, as they did hers.

A faint smile played over Cat's lips. Tara was not
totally her father's clone. There was a lot of her in her
daughter. Cat repeated her question.

The little girl spoke up quickly. "At school today."

"What?" Cat's eyes widened in shock. The term was
one she'd never expected to hear being bandied about at
an elementary-school class, even if it was one for gifted
students. "Who said it?"

"Tessa's mommy." Tara's face tightened in concentration before she resumed. "Tessa left her favorite book
behind, and I went out to give it to her before she got
in the car. I heard her mommy say to Stephen's mommy
that Tessa's daddy was a 'real bastard.' What did she
mean?" Tara asked, her eyes wide with inquiry.

Relief eased Cat's tense muscles. The woman hadn't
been referring to Tara. Mrs. Saunders was obviously going through another rough patch with her ex-husband,
and Tara had overheard the tirade.

"Tessa's mother was angry with Tessa's father, and
she called him a name," Cat replied, her tone soothing.

Tara, undaunted, wouldn't allow this to rest until her

inquisitiveness was satisfied. "But what does it mean? Should I get my dictionary and look it up?"

The realization that she wasn't going to escape Tara's probing forced Cat's hand. "It's a grown-up term." Then, knowing she couldn't stall any longer, Cat added, "Tessa's mother used it to mean a not very nice person. Do you understand?"

The little girl nodded her head, the simple explanation accepted. Wrapping her soft arms around her mother's neck, Tara planted a smacking kiss on Cat's cheek.

"Can I go and play now?"

Cat returned the kiss, happy that Tara seemed satisfied with the definition she'd given her. "Scoot," she said, and the little girl eagerly complied.

Cat stood up, watching as Tara dashed out of the room. This was too close a call for her liking. So far Tara hadn't really asked too many questions about her lack of a father, probably because she had several stable male influences in her life, among them her grandfather and her uncle, who stepped in when needed. And, the world being what it was, there were several other children she knew being raised in single-parent homes.

But still, the day would come when her daughter would demand to know the truth. A truth she had a right to know. Cat only hoped that Tara would understand her reasons for keeping it hidden.

And what would she say to her daughter when that day came? There would never be time or words enough to fully prepare. How could she ever make her child understand her motives? How could she tell her daughter that she'd been a fool for love? Would Tara ever comprehend? Or forgive?

Cat straightened her slim shoulders and poured herself a fresh cup of coffee. She sipped it slowly, savoring the warmth of the hot liquid as it flowed through her on this unexpectedly crisp, early-September day.

Restless, she decided to check and see if the mail had come yet, as it usually arrived early on Saturday.

Pulling on a navy cardigan sweater over her long-sleeved white oxford shirt to ward off the chill, Cat walked in silent concentration to the mailbox at the end of her driveway. She paused to watch a pair of scampering red squirrels, who dashed up and down one of the large evergreens, chasing away a twice-as-big gray squirrel in the process. She stood for a minute and observed the songbirds that crowded the hanging bird feeder, all eager to eat.

If only life could be as simple, she thought as she gathered the mail and then reentered the house.

But it wasn't and never would be.

Cat dropped the pile of mail onto the kitchen table. Among the assorted bills, catalogs and magazines was a formal-looking envelope bearing the imprint of her alma mater, Cedar Hill University.

She put down her coffee cup and grabbed a knife from the nearby drawer, slit open the envelope and quickly scanned the contents. Color drained from her face. Hoping that she had read the invitation wrong, Cat carefully reread it.

No, she hadn't made a mistake; the invitation was all too clear, all too real. It was a request for her presence at a reception to be given in two weeks to welcome the newest member of the Cedar Hill faculty, who would be heading up the newly created Department of Celtic Studies.

Cat dropped to the kitchen chair, the note clutched in her hand, the impact of the words hitting her like a body blow. *He* was coming back, back after all these years.

Sweet saints in heaven, she thought, her other hand over her mouth as if to stifle a gasp. *Why now?*

She forced herself to take a deep breath. Of course she couldn't go to the welcome party. It was impossible.

Smoothing out the crushed vellum sheet, her index finger traced the fancy calligraphied letters of his name. Suddenly, Cat began to tremble; tears formed in her green eyes.

It was only a name. What harm could come from a name?

But, her heart countered, there was a man behind the name, a man to be reckoned with.

Feelings that were buried under layers of pain and heartache, which she thought she'd put behind her in the past where they belonged, rose unexpectedly to the surface, clogging her memory.

And what about her daughter?

A rising tide of fear shot through Cat. Had he somehow discovered that their brief love affair had produced a child?

So what if he had? she thought, taking a sip of the now-cooling coffee. Tara was *her* daughter, hers alone. She'd borne her, raised her, loved her—been all the parent the little girl had ever needed. Seen Tara through upset stomachs and scraped knees. Been there for her through bad dreams and rainy afternoons. Read countless stories and answered thousands of "whys."

Besides, Cat was no longer the vulnerable young woman that she had been, easily swept away by the dashing Rory Sullivan's abundant charm and good looks. It wouldn't work a second time. Her heart was secure, impervious to its former follies. Time and distance had repaired the cracks, cauterized the wounds.

Or had they?

Rising, she grabbed the wall phone and tapped out the RSVP number, quickly conveying her sincere regrets that she wouldn't be able to attend.

Cat hung up the phone and leaned against the counter, her head bowed. She remained that way for several minutes before raising her head and wiping away the traces of tears that wet her cheeks. She couldn't afford to waste time on the past; she had a business to run, a life of her own to lead. And, most importantly, it wouldn't do for Tara to find her like this. Her daughter came before everything, including regrets.

Sleep was impossible that night.

Cat tossed and turned, unable to find the comfort and peace that she craved. She should be too tired to be awake. It had been a busy day at the bookstore, with a large shipment of inventory to unpack and put away. Her muscles ached, yearning for the restorative power of total rest.

However, her mind had other plans.

Cat turned on the lamp by her bed and sat up, glancing at the clock. She knew what the problem was. *Memories*. Ever since that fancy envelope ripped open the tenuous hold she maintained over her thoughts on the past, the magnetic pull of recollections gripped her senses, nudging aside her hunger for sleep, for forgetfulness.

It had been almost seven years since she had seen the father of her child. Even though he was no longer a part of her personal life, he was still very much a part of her professional life. Because of the popular history books that he'd written, books that she carried in her store, that fact was inescapable. His sharp black-and-white photograph adorned dust jackets: He was the quintessentially handsome, brilliant college professor, a man of undeniable magnetism and taste who could wear, she recalled, a tuxedo or jeans with equal aplomb. The kind of drop-dead-gorgeous looks that constantly stirred and fluttered female hearts—and would until his dying day.

Frustrated, Cat threw back the fluffy white comforter, leaving the bed that offered her no sanctuary from the seductive rush of memories. Slipping on her comfortable hunter-green chenille robe, she padded barefoot to her cozy kitchen for a soothing cup of hot chocolate.

While waiting for the water to boil, she looked out the window over the sink to the sky, touched by a splattering of diamond-chipped stars.

She had thought that he'd been like them: brilliant, remote, out of her reach.

The kettle's whistle signaled to her that the water was ready. Cat poured the boiling liquid over the cocoa mix, her free hand automatically reaching for a spoon and stirring the contents of the mug. Her mind dwelled on the fact that the unthinkable had happened, that without her having to reach for them, the dreams, the fantasies, had come to her.

And that's all they were, she thought as she sipped the rich taste of the chocolate. *Fantasies.*

Without foundation. Without strength. Nothing to build upon, she sadly acknowledged. First love had swept her away on a tide of rising emotions, breaking through the barriers around her heart. She could see it all so clearly: He was again the instructor, she the willing student.

Her memory slipped back, caught in the seductive web of the past....

Cat was running late, the result of having gotten stuck in traffic. Today of all days, she thought as she pulled her car into the small parking lot that adjoined the reconverted barn that housed her bookstore and gift shop.

She'd been open less than a year, and this was her first really big event, hosting a signing of an important new book. All her hard work lobbying the small-press publisher had paid off. She had the first appearance of a man who was getting extensive, glowing media coverage for his introductory foray into the crowded field of historical writing. After reading an advanced copy of the book, Cat had been determined to get the author in her store, especially since he was teaching a semester at Cedar Hill. So impressed was she by his stirring command of words that she wanted to share her enthusiasm with the public. She and her assistant had sent out invitations to a select mailing list, then crossed their fingers that all the people who had responded affirmatively would show up.

Cat finally relaxed about a half hour later after making sure all the details were taken care of: that she had enough chairs to hold the people rapidly filling the store, that the coffee and tea were ready, and that the small iced cookies and cupcakes her assistant, Mary Alice, had picked up from a local bakery were set out. She checked the small pine table holding the large stack of books, fussing with the display until she had it just right.

She chatted with a few of her regular customers while they waited for the author to show up. Several of them had already purchased the book on her recommendation earlier in the week and were as anxious as she was to meet the writer.

Still, Cat was totally unprepared for the shock that hit her squarely in the chest when the door opened several minutes later, and the author sauntered in.

He was the handsomest man she had ever seen. Photographs, she realized, didn't completely do him justice. Tall, whipcord lean, he entered the room like a conquering prince of old, pride stamped indelibly on the aristocratic planes of his face. Casually dressed in a pale blue oxford shirt and tight indigo jeans, topped by a black leather jacket, Cat couldn't take her eyes off him.

She was instantly mesmerized by the brilliant blue of his eyes, deep and dark, as he looked in her direction. Kerry blue to be sure, surrounded by thick dark lashes many women would envy, and curving black eyebrows. Black hair, thick and slightly wavy, fell to his nape. His mouth was wide with a sensually full lower lip.

And then he smiled. Caitlyn saw his mouth quirk to one side, a dimple evident in one cheek, the white flash of his teeth glowed against his lightly tanned skin.

She watched as he brushed away a stray lock of hair from his forehead. His fingers were long and slender. A silver Claddagh ring gleamed on his right hand.

Unbidden and quite unexpected came the thought—what would those hands feel like on her body?

Like heaven, she answered her own question, imagining the outcome.

Heat flushed her cheeks as she realized the sensual path her mind was taking.

Apologizing for his tardiness, he quietly introduced himself to Cat, whose heart started to pound deep in her chest. She introduced him to the crowd, then stepped back to let him begin.

She, along with the assembled customers, was enthralled both by the sound of his voice and by the subject matter he discussed. He made history come alive, as if he were relating events that happened just yesterday instead of centuries ago.

With a will of their own, her eyes returned to feast

on him. A poet, a warrior-king, a rebel; all these things and more Cat saw mirrored in his compelling face. His was a countenance that personified all that was masculine and beautiful, all that was heroic about the Irish.

The day was a huge success. The cash register hummed with activity as close to a hundred copies of the book were sold. People lined up to chat with the author, some, Cat noted, shamelessly flirting.

He seemed to take it all in stride, staying later, making sure everyone who wanted a signed copy got one.

A few customers still milled about the store, talking and adding items to their planned purchases while Cat straightened up.

"Miss Kildare?"

She almost dropped the empty china plate she was holding when he spoke. "Yes?"

"Any more left?"

"I beg your pardon?"

"Of the cookies or the cupcakes?"

"Sorry, no," she responded. "Looks like the food was as big as hit as you were, Dr. Sullivan."

He smiled. "Rory, please."

Her tongue snaked out to wet her suddenly dry lips.

He checked the watch on his right wrist. "It's well past lunch and a bit early for dinner, but I'm rather hungry. What about you?"

Cat hadn't eaten since a hastily grabbed breakfast this morning, and while she was indeed hungry, not to mention intrigued at the thought of sharing a meal with this man, she had a business to run. "Thanks for the offer, but I really can't. There's too much to do here."

Mary Alice entered the conversation, not having missed the intense looks her boss had given their guest speaker. "I can close up today, Cat."

Cat threw her assistant a grateful glance. "You're sure? You were scheduled to leave in half an hour."

"No problem. I'll just make a phone call and let my husband know I'll be home later."

"Thanks."

"It's settled then," Rory added, waiting while Cat gathered her purse and gave a few last-minute instructions to her assistant. When Cat joined him, he leaned close to her and whispered, "I know a wonderful place not far from here."

That was the beginning.

Time flew by with dinners, lunches, or whatever moments could be snatched from both their busy schedules. Cat discovered that unlike her, Rory was an only child, born to older parents who indulged him until their death while he was in his junior year of college. She listened while he outlined his ambitions, his plans for the future, filed away details as she was drawn deeper and deeper into his private circle.

Then, one morning, not many weeks after they first began seeing one another, Cat awoke with the certain knowledge that she was in love with him. She had been from the first day they'd met. It was a fact that she couldn't deny any longer. His charming good looks and exciting mind had stolen her heart, yet what would come of it? she asked herself. There were far more intriguing women on campus he could have, faculty and students alike. Women more experienced and sophisticated than she, who knew how to play the game of love. Women willing to break the rules for an opportunity to share his bed.

With so many available choices, why would he ever look in her direction?

The amazing fact, to her, was that he had. Or maybe

she was reading far too much into their friendship. He had yet to even kiss her.

She had barely arrived at her bookstore one day when there was a knock on the door about an hour before she was due to open. "Hello. Cat?"

It was him. There was no mistaking that voice, his distinctive manner of speaking. Without hesitation, she unlocked the door and let him in.

He was casually dressed, looking absurdly elegant in his relaxed fashion. His short-sleeved blue chambray shirt was open at the neck minus a tie, revealing a sprinkle of black hair, and was tucked into a pair of faded jeans that hugged his slim hips and long legs.

She'd had to fight back the almost overwhelming inclination she had to reach out her hand and open the rest of the buttons to see for herself if that hair covered his entire chest or was just a dusting.

He stood before her, a pleased, triumphant smile on his firm mouth.

"What?" she'd asked in response to that look.

"I needed to do something this morning," he said, stepping closer to her and closing the door with a firm click. "Something I've longed to do for so many weeks that I thought I would explode from the wait."

Cat was caught by the steely strength of his fingers, which wrapped gently around her upper arms. She was brought quickly into intimate contact with his lean, hard body. His black head dipped and his wickedly beautiful mouth met her own with a searing passion that shook Cat to the core of her being.

Again and again his mouth swept over hers, cajoling, demanding, seeking, persuading. It was a series of messages she couldn't ignore. Her wildest fantasies were coming true. Cat gave herself up to the hungry possession of his kisses, linking her arms around his neck, holding on and drawing him closer as she willingly surrendered.

"My God," Rory whispered when he finally broke off the kiss, his breathing ragged. He held her close to his chest, stroking one hand up and down her back in a soothing motion, kissing the top of her head.

Cat could only smile. The dreams she hadn't dared to hope for were quickly becoming reality.

Rory lifted her chin so that she could see his face. "Can you get away this weekend?"

"What for?" she'd asked, her heart still beating faster than normal.

"I've managed to rent a place down the shore. Very nice and quite private, I've been told. We'd have the beach all to ourselves. How about it?"

Cat stepped away from his embrace, needing perspective while she thought over his invitation. She understood what he was asking. It was there in his eyes; it had flavored his kisses. Why not go with him? Hadn't these past weeks shown that she could trust him? He hadn't pushed their relationship farther than she was comfortable with.

Besides, unable to stop herself from glancing in his direction, she loved him. And loving, she knew, meant eventually expressing that love in the most intimate way possible.

She reached out her hand to take his. "Yes." With that decision made, Cat realized she had burned her bridges and crossed the threshold.

The look in his dark blue eyes banished any lingering trepidation she felt. "You won't regret this, Cat." He kissed her softly and sweetly on her still-swollen mouth. "I promise."

Four days later Cat inhaled the salt-tinged air as she walked upon the upper deck of the large glass, wood and stone house. She and Rory had spent a relaxing day swimming, sunbathing, and later, shopping in a local antiques store.

The brilliant sun was low in the sky, suspended over the horizon. Snatching up her camera from a nearby chair, Cat snapped a picture, wanting to capture a slice of this day so that she could relive it later, though she suspected that no picture could truly capture what she was feeling.

Happiness bubbled up inside her, threatening to spill over.

The French door that led from the upstairs living room opened, and she heard Rory behind her, welcomed the strong arm that he slid so possessively around her waist. She could feel the heat of his bare chest through her thin cotton tank top. His jeans-clad legs felt hard against the exposed length of hers, covered only in shorts. Slowly, seductively, his left hand curved around her throat, caressing her neck and shoulder.

She wanted to suspend this moment in time. From the open door she could hear the sweet flow of an alto saxophone emanating from the expensive stereo system. She listened, swaying to the soothing, seductive rhythm. A slow sensation of heat arose within her.

When his mouth, sweet with wine, captured hers in a kiss potently powerful, Cat gave in willingly. This was the moment of surrender. Her heart knew it. Her body demanded it.

So did he.

Bending, Rory lifted her in his strong arms, carrying her through the house until he reached the bedroom that had been his alone last night.

He set her down, his lips still locked possessively with hers before he pulled back.

Cat was surprised. She could have easily kissed him for days on end, so exciting was the mating of their mouths.

When Rory finally spoke, his words were delivered in a soft, husky tone. "I want to see all of you, Cat. Now. Will you do that for me?"

The light in the room was beginning to fade. She watched as her lover-to-be slipped into the enveloping shadows while she remained in the glow of the setting sun as it sank in glorious splendor through the windows. Colors streaked the sky, giving her a backdrop touched with the beauty only nature could paint.

Wetting her lips, she took a deep breath. Slowly, she pulled the white top over her head, revealing pale, creamy skin. Next, she reached around and unsnapped her lacy bra, letting it fall to the floor.

A growing sense of power, like a charge of electricity, flowed through her. He was giving her the choice. With a smile, she unzipped her white shorts, peeling them, along with her serviceable white, French-cut panties, down her legs.

Her task done, Cat stood, her back straight, her manner proud.

"Your hair, loosen it," came the softly spoken command.

Cat removed the clip that held her hair, threading her slender fingers through it, fluffing it around her shoulders. It was thick, wavy, with streaks of gold among the deep auburn tresses.

The room was suddenly flooded with light as Rory

turned on the lamp that rested on the nightstand. He'd been sitting in an overstuffed low chair.

He stood, slowly dispensing with his faded denims, letting them fall to his feet. His fingers hooked into the trim blue briefs he wore, pushed them aside.

Her voice sounded strained as her eyes opened wide, riveted by the sight of him. Better than any photograph, more striking than a marble statue, he was, to her, perfection. "I've never..." Her words trailed off as he crossed the room.

He cupped her cheek, whispering, "Hush, my sweet love. I know." Then, gentle as a breeze off the ocean, he traced a finger along her throat, across her collarbone, then came to the swell of her breasts. His large hand lightly caressed her flesh. As if he had forever, he continued to discover the wonderful secrets of her body, molding, shaping, exploring, leading her on the journey.

Then, he welcomed her participation. "Touch me," he said, his voice deep and demanding.

Cat complied, exalting in the feel of the crisp black hair that angled across his lean, muscular chest. She stroked his rib cage, palmed her hand across his flat belly. Felt the power in his strong thighs as her fingertips glided down and over them.

Then, needing to experience the taste, the touch of his lips again, she sought his mouth with her own, letting the growing hunger that twisted her insides speak for her.

In turn, Rory responded with a primitive fervor that drew her deeper and deeper into a vortex of indescribable passion.

Cat's initiation into total womanhood was accomplished with gentleness and love, with sharing and joy.

Another month passed rapidly, with Cat wrapped in a

haze of love and what she thought was security. Any day he would ask her to marry him, share his life as she shared his love, she was sure of that.

Then, late one afternoon the dreamworld she'd lived in disintegrated when he shared his news with her. Snuggled in his bed, replete after intense lovemaking, Rory explained the offer he'd just received.

"It's a dream come true, Cat, something I've been working for. The opportunity to further my studies at Trinity College in Dublin with a prestigious research fellowship." His voice sang with delight as he hugged Cat close, one hand stroking her tousled hair.

"It's all so sudden," she'd heard herself say.

"Yes, but so what? I applied over a year ago, and it's finally come through. My flight to Dublin leaves this weekend, and I've already given notice to Cedar Hill that I won't be returning for the fall term. I'll take care of finding us a place to live," he announced. "Then, when you've said your goodbyes here, you can join me, only don't make it too long, darling."

Cat listened to his voice brimming with excitement. Suddenly her hopes for the future, *their* future, were vanishing, washed away by the waves of his plans like grains of sand.

"I can't."

"What do you mean, you *can't?*"

"Just that," Cat said, each word pulled from her like a layer of skin being removed. "I can't give up my life and go to Ireland with you on a whim."

"Whim? Is that what you think this is?"

"Maybe not for you."

He stiffened beside her.

"This is obviously what you want." She knew he was ambitious. She accepted that. Or at least she thought she had. But the idea of uprooting herself was unthinkable. Just pack up her life and go, without a care for her family, her friends, the business she loved and worked so hard to build? There were so many reasons why she couldn't go, but he'd never thought to ask.

"I thought you loved me."

"I do." And she did, so much so that she felt sick at having to refuse him. Ireland? She wanted to go there someday. But she couldn't go now. Couldn't walk away from all she had here.

His voice was low and soft. "Then come with me."

"And do what?"

"Be with me."

She reiterated, "And do what?"

"Whatever you like."

His arrogant words chilled her, sending icy tentacles to wrap around her heart.

"I can't do that. I have a business to run."

"It's not like I'm asking you to forget about it," he said. "Just set it aside for a little while. Get someone else, like Mary Alice, to handle it for you."

Just set it aside. Like it was a toy or a game she could easily pick up later when the mood struck. "For how long?"

He shrugged. "I don't know. A year. Maybe more."

"Then my answer is still no."

Rory threw back the sheet and rose from the bed. He stood facing her, naked, like a Celtic warrior getting ready for battle. "You won't change your mind?"

Sadness choked Cat's voice. "No."

She watched him dress with quick, economical movements, feeling her happiness wither inside her, shriveling in the sudden chill.

Rory walked back to where she lay. His eyes, once

warm and tender, now resembled cold, frostbitten chips of dark blue ice. "I won't ask again."

"I know," she admitted, holding back the tears until he left the room. Sobs shook her body repeatedly. He never once mentioned marriage. Stupidly, she assumed that he wanted it because she had. Couldn't he understand that she couldn't throw her dreams into limbo merely to be his live-in love with no guarantees? Her dreams were important to her. Foolishly, she'd believed that they were to him also. And, she was too proud to beg him to make the ultimate commitment when it was obvious that's not what he had in mind.

Cat rinsed out her cup and set it in the sink, then wiped away the hot tears that welled in her eyes.

The secure world that she'd built for herself and her child was about to be invaded.

The man who'd broken her heart was coming back.

Chapter Two

Finally, he was, he believed, back where he truly belonged.

After almost seven years of voluntary exile in Ireland, Rory Sullivan had returned to the States. Returned not to the elegant four-story town house on the Upper East Side of New York City where he was born and raised and which he now owned, but instead to Cedar Hill, the small town in southeastern Pennsylvania where he had taught college. Back to a fresh start at a new life. Back to a place overflowing with memories.

He held one such in his hand, a slim volume of poetry. It was an old book, privately published and quite rare, bound in leather and stamped in gold, a find from an estate sale; it was a unique birthday gift he had cherished doubly because of the person who had given it to him. Contained inside the pages were poems of love and longing, of heartbreak and happiness, the work of an Irish woman in the late nineteenth century, simply titled *To My Beloved.*

He gently opened the book, read the inscription that he'd read hundreds of times before: *Always and forever, Cat.*

The irony of that phrase haunted him. Just because you left a place, or a person, didn't mean they left you. Some memories were burned too deep to ever depart; they remained in your mind, constant reminders of what was.

What was, what is, what would always be for him— the woman whose memory he'd tried to ignore. A recollection he'd tried—but found impossible—to suppress. A woman that he tried his damnedest to erase from the deepest recesses of his mind and found she was unforgettable. The passion he tried to so hard to bury where he thought it belonged—in the over-and-done-with category—was ultimately unquenchable.

She was still there. In his heart. In his mind. In his past. A living ghost that had attached itself to him with ethereal chains stronger than any forged with steel.

One day several months ago, while surfing the Internet in his Dublin apartment, he'd stumbled upon her name quite by accident. He'd been checking a list of specialty Irish bookstores in the States, trying to locate an out-of-print research book. It was available in two places, one of which turned out to be hers. Cat's bookstore had its own Web site, and it included a recent article from a local newspaper on her thriving business, along with a current photo that showed a beautiful woman who looked barely older than some of his undergraduate students. Even through the filter of a monitor screen her hair still gleamed that particular shade of reddish brown. A color he could never forget—gold-dusted cinnamon.

He didn't need a closer inspection to recall the exact shade of her eyes; their color was imprinted in his memory. Green. The green of a ripe lime in summer.

Once, while searching through an antiques shop in the Irish capital, he'd found two items that mirrored that shade. A lady's antique-gold brooch that held a stunning emerald in the center and a pair of matching gentleman's Edwardian cuff links, which he wore tonight with his tuxedo. He'd bought both items on the spot, unable to resist, because they reminded him of her.

Was there someone special in her life now? he wondered. Someone who'd replaced him in her heart, her mind, her bed? The article had given no personal details.

Who was he kidding? Rory thought. Of course there had to be someone else. He'd been gone a long time. Too long to believe he'd find her waiting patiently for a man who'd walked out on her.

And why should she? He'd foolishly slammed the door on their relationship. Forced her to make a choice.

And she had.

A choice he'd had to live with.

Until now.

Had she ever regretted that decision? Had she ever wished that she'd chosen a life with him instead of her business? Did she ever spare a random thought for *what if?*

Rory raked a hand through his fashionably cut dark hair, then loosened the black tie he wore and poured himself a whiskey, neat, from the Waterford decanter that rested on a small butler's table in the living room of his rented condo. The strong taste was a sharp contrast to the two glasses of champagne he'd consumed at his welcome party, thrown in his honor tonight by university colleagues. A party he'd hoped she would have attended.

But she hadn't. Throughout the night he'd watched and waited, in vain. Cat never showed, even after he'd made sure that she was invited.

Payback time?

No, the Cat he remembered wouldn't have blown him off for petty reasons. That wasn't her style.

Then why didn't she attend?

Maybe she had better things to do, he mused as he prowled about the room. Better places to be. Or perhaps she didn't want any part in this prodigal's return.

That thought left a particularly bad taste in his mouth, so he poured himself another whiskey to wash it away.

Had he made a colossal mistake coming back here? Several other colleges and universities had wanted him to teach at their campuses. Had wooed him with fabulous promises and tempting offers.

But they lacked proximity to what he was seeking.

His friends and fellow professors in Ireland asked him to reconsider when he'd informed them he was leaving. Stay where you belong, they urged. Settle down with one woman and raise a family, a proper *Irish* family. Past time, they argued, that he had a wife and children.

But he couldn't. Much as he loved Dublin and the country of his ancestors, it wasn't truly home.

Home really *was,* Rory had found out in the ensuing years, where the heart resided. And his had been left behind, in the soft hands of one Miss Caitlyn Kildare. The time had come to see if it could be reclaimed, or if it was lost forever.

Reaching into his inside jacket pocket, Rory withdrew his wallet. He flipped it open, stared at the photo encased in soft plastic inside. It was an old picture, a worn, faded snapshot that showed signs of handling. A woman's face.

Drawing it from its protective haven, Rory smoothed out the edges, his fingers caressing the picture.

Back then nothing had come between him and his ambition. He hadn't needed anyone or anything in his life distracting him from his goal.

Or so he'd thought. Love was a name people gave to sugarcoat the intensity of physical desire. Love gave permission to act on those desires, to indulge without guilt. It was pleasant, but in most cases temporary. Enjoyable while it lasted, but nothing to take seriously.

That's what he'd told himself.

He naively, or stupidly, believed that when he left Caitlyn for the life he wanted in Ireland she would eventually disappear from his thoughts, that his desire for her would evaporate with the distance and the years that separated them.

Rory's mouth quirked into a mocking grin as he removed the tie and unfastened several buttons on his pleated white tuxedo shirt. Easy to think. Harder to accomplish.

Even with an ocean dividing them, she was constantly with him. He discovered that he carried her within his heart, and his heart refused to allow the memories to die. Instead, it constantly fed him slices of remembrances, doled out carefully at times when he least expected them. In the solitude of his apartment in Dublin, he found himself reaching for her at night, only to find empty space in his bed. Working on a manuscript, he would raise his head, ready to tell her something, to share a fact or an idea, to get her reaction. Only emptiness met his sweeping look. Silence and memories. Echoes of a time past.

Once he'd even attempted to eradicate the specter of

her by sleeping with another woman. Deliberately, he'd chosen a woman who reminded him of Cat. A green-eyed, red-haired woman. So what if her eyes lacked the glowing polish of emeralds shot with sunlight? What did it matter if her hair didn't possess the fire or scent of Cat's? Lemon-scented, burnished flame belonged to Cat alone.

His experiment was a horrible failure. It wasn't the woman's fault, he admitted to himself. She had no way of knowing that she was only a substitute for the real thing, a copy that never quite measured up to the original.

With hindsight, Rory could admit that he'd put his body into the act of sex, but not his heart. His performance may have been instinctively accurate and consummately skilled, yet it lacked a certain fire, a brilliance that transcended the simple and made it sublime. It lacked what he'd had with Cat. Conviction. Rightness. Beauty.

Rory reflected on how much easier it was to analyze that now. Love was the missing ingredient, the special spice that elevated the giving of pleasure to the mingling of souls. It had taken him precious time to recognize and accept that fact.

But was it too late? Too late to return and recapture what he'd thrown away all those years ago? He stared at the face in the photograph, at the deep, delightful smile and the welcoming eyes.

Maybe it wasn't. Maybe second chances did exist.

Always and forever.

He was damn sure going to give it a try. After all, he had nothing to lose. Nothing that he hadn't already lost once before.

Rory smiled as he returned the photo to his wallet. If

there was one thing he was good at, it was getting what he wanted when he set his mind to it.

And Caitlyn Kildare was what he wanted.

No doubts.

No hesitations.

No questions.

So, he wasn't going to let a little thing like a no-show at his party deter him from pursuing his quarry. He'd come too far and waited too long.

Besides, he thought as he climbed the winding stairs that led up to his bedroom, tomorrow was soon enough to begin his campaign.

"A dozen roses in a Waterford vase. Someone's sure got extravagant taste," Mary Alice commented after the florist's delivery van departed. She bent and sniffed the bouquet, which adorned the checkout counter. "Hmm," she murmured, "a lovely scent." She straightened and threw a questioning glance in Cat's direction. "So, who are they from? The lawyer or the doctor?"

"Neither."

"Someone new then?"

Cat shrugged. "I haven't a clue."

"No note?"

"None whatsoever."

"Then how do you know that one of them didn't send it?"

Cat moved from behind the counter and whisked the feather duster over a small spin-around display of post-cards. "There's no reason for either one to send me flowers," she explained to her assistant. "I haven't seen George since he was transferred to the D.A.'s office in Philly during the summer. Paul has such an erratic schedule at the hospital, and since I'm a mother with a young child I doubt we'll be seeing much of one another in the future.''

"No sparks?' Mary Alice asked.

Cat paused before she answered, choosing her words carefully. "They're both *nice* guys, I enjoyed going out with them, and I like them. But it will never be anything more.''

"That's too bad,'' the older woman stated. "I know that your mom and brother will be disappointed, seeing how they both set you up with their colleagues.''

Cat smiled. "Mom and Brendan both want me to be happy, and neither like to take no for an answer, which is why I humored them. And it's been a long time since I'd gone out on a date.''

"But they weren't *him.*''

Cat stopped her dusting. "Him who?''

"Tara's father.''

"He doesn't enter into this at all.''

"You're certain?''

"Yes.''

"Well—'' Mary Alice paused, giving Cat a knowing glance "—I'm not so sure about that.''

"I am,'' Cat insisted.

Mary Alice wisely let the subject drop. "But it still doesn't answer who sent you the flowers.''

"Maybe a customer.''

"Extravagant gesture for a customer.''

"Remember Mrs. O'Malley who brought me back that lovely Aran Isle sweater when she went to Ireland last year?''

"That's different, Cat. You paid her for it.''

Cat ignored her friend's comment. "Or it could have been Mr. Boyle. You know he doesn't get out anymore since his accident, and I send him his favorite magazines and a new book each month.''

Mary Alice shook her head and lowered her voice as a customer walked into the shop. ''It's not from a grateful customer, I'll wager. More like a lover, or a man who hopes to be, I'm thinking.''

''Well, being as I don't have one right now or plans in the immediate future, that's not likely,'' Cat responded, greeting the new arrival with a friendly smile.

''And whose fault is that?''

Cat shot her assistant a dark look, then relaxed as she saw the grin on Mary Alice's face. She rolled her eyes and then turned back to her customer. ''May I help you find something, ma'am?'' she asked.

''Yes,'' the woman replied. ''I'm looking for that new biography on Lady Gregory. There was a review in this past Sunday's *Inquirer*.''

Cat glanced up from her desk where she was working on sorting out several special orders for customers as a cold finger of apprehension touched her spine. She couldn't identify the source, yet it was there, like a blast of cool air.

Couldn't or wouldn't identify? she wondered.

Rory.

Rory, her brain echoed in a remembered litany of passion and pain. *Why is it that every time I think I'm almost over you there is always something there to remind me?*

Because, she answered herself, as long as she had Tara there would always be a reminder. Daily. Constant. In a look, or in the way Tara tilted her head. Then there was that smile. Her father's smile.

Damn you, Rory, Cat thought. Damn you for my greatest pleasure and my deepest hell. Damn you once more for making me remember all the moments we spent together.

Had he sent the flowers?

And if he had, for what purpose? To confuse and confound her? To let her know she was in his thoughts?

He could do that in person if he wanted.

Would she be ready?

Cat reluctantly admitted that she would never be quite ready, still maybe it would be for the best. Get it over with, quick and clean. Simple. She had survived his leaving; she would survive his coming back again. Besides, she had nothing in common with him anyway.

Except a child, came the sadly sweet thought. A beautiful little girl created out of the love they had shared.

Correction, her inner voice added, out of the love *she* had for him. But that love was over. In the past. The fire was dead. Ashes were all that remained. And wasn't it better that way? Being consumed by the flames was no way to live. Charred fragments of her heart had survived once. Now it was cloaked in self-induced asbestos to keep it safe. Maybe someday she would love again. A nice, sweet, gentle love. The kind that was comfortable and secure. Nothing that heated the blood or scorched the soul.

Been there, she thought. Done that. Don't plan on making that mistake ever again.

Her glance fell to the silver-framed photograph that rested on her desk, sharing space with piles of papers, a computer and books. It was of her and Tara, smiling broadly to the camera. Taken at her daughter's last birthday party.

He'd missed them all. All the cakes, the presents, the laughter, and most especially the fun of seeing the wonder and excitement of a birthday through a child's eyes.

But it couldn't be helped. Or regretted.

The intercom on her phone buzzed, giving Cat a good excuse to put her mind on something else.

Rory sat in his leased car in the parking lot of Cat's bookstore, remembering the first time he'd come here. Flush with success at the rave notices his initial effort had produced, he'd been excited to do his first real book signing and thrilled to finally meet the woman who'd sent such a glowing review to his publisher. He recalled the shock that first hit him as he walked through the door of The Silver Harp—he'd been expecting a much older woman to be the owner. Instead, she'd been closer to his own age, he discovered, twenty-five to his thirty.

And lovely beyond compare. A dew-dappled apricot rose with a hint of a blush. That's the flower he associated with her. The flower he'd sent today.

She was smart. Funny. More than able to meet him halfway. A woman who stirred him on so many levels. A woman of passion, honesty and conviction.

He watched as several people walked in and out, some with small bags, a few with large.

So what was he waiting for? He wasn't going to get a damn thing accomplished by sitting in his car and staring at the continual flow of customers.

Rory got out and locked the car with a click of his key ring. A few steps took him to the door of the stone building, where he turned the brass handle and stepped inside.

She'd made a few changes in the interim years. Soft strains of Celtic music now played in the background. A subtle fragrance hung in the air, light and spicy, making him think of golden autumn days and crisp fall nights, of colors he associated with Cat. A wooden display on a nearby bare pine table held store newsletters. Rory picked one up and perused it. Poetry readings, book signings, storytelling hour for children, an upcoming Irish step-dancing demonstration. Something for everyone.

"Hi. May I help you?"

Rory turned his head at the sound of the female voice.

"Oh my, it's Professor Sullivan, isn't it?" Mary Alice said, her eyes widening in surprise.

Rory smiled. "I'm flattered that you remembered me."

"Let's say that you made an impression that doesn't soon fade," Mary Alice responded wryly.

"Really?" he responded with a lift of one black eyebrow. "How very sweet of you to say that."

"I'd only be speaking the truth."

"Does Caitlyn Kildare still own this place?"

"She sure does."

"Is she by any chance here today?"

"Yes."

"Then would you tell her that I'd like to see her."

Mary Alice nodded her head. "Just you wait right here, and I'll go and let her know that you've come to say hello. There's freshly brewed tea and coffee if you'd like something to drink." With a wave of her hand she indicated a sturdy pine sideboard upon which sat a coffeemaker and next to it a carafe of hot water. "There's a few things to nibble on if you'd like, too. Personally, I'd try the shortbread. One taste and you swear you've died and been reborn."

"That good?"

"Better than almost anything," she insisted.

Rory almost laughed at that declaration. He'd tasted a few things in his time that would have put the shortbread treat to shame, he was sure. One of them had been Cat's skin. Smooth as cream. And her mouth, sweet as honey.

His body stirred achingly with the sensory pictures his mind painted. Images grown sharper. Clearer. Especially now that he allowed himself to see them freely. Artists had a term for that which resurfaced after being buried under layers of paint—pentimento. The discovery of the treasure beneath the surface, beneath the obvious.

As for coffee or tea, he didn't need further stimulation. Thinking about Cat was stimulating enough. Much more than enough.

Mary Alice slipped into the back room and closed the door behind her.

Cat glanced up from her computer screen when her assistant entered.

"You've got a visitor," the older woman announced in a soft voice.

A sudden chill ran along Cat's spine. She asked the question to which she had already guessed the answer. "Who?"

"Rory Sullivan."

Cat momentarily shifted her eyes to the picture of her daughter, then forced them away as she saved the document that she was working on and closed down the machine.

"Do you want me to show him in here?"

"No," Cat replied quickly. "Would you mind telling him that I'll be out in a few minutes?"

"Sure."

As Mary Alice turned to go, Cat spoke again. "Has he..." She was going to say "changed," but opted against finishing the question. She would know soon enough herself. "Never mind."

Mary Alice left and Cat stood up, walked a few feet to the bathroom, flicked on the light and checked her face in the mirror. She filled a small paper cup with cold water from the tap and swallowed it. Most of her lipstick was gone so she reached into the pocket of her skirt and ran the tube of plain lip gloss across her mouth.

All ready.

Who was she kidding? she thought. Certainly not herself. She was far from ready. Miles away from okay. Light-years from calm. But she had to do this, now. Bite the bullet. Face the music. And all the other clichés she could think of.

All the intervening years melted away, and the past rose up from behind the shuttered wall of her memory, released and living, standing before her when she walked onto the sales floor.

Across the width of the room, as if he could feel her presence, Rory turned and their eyes met.

If Cat thought he was handsome before, she marveled at how much the years had improved his features. Mature, polished, elegant, he was all that, but harder, Cat noted. There was a toughness, a steely strength underlying the facile good looks, obviously dormant when she knew him. Now there was no denying the beautiful arrogance of his face or his eyes. Those enticing Kerry-blue eyes. Just like the old song. Smiling Irish eyes that could, and did, steal your heart away. But in the stealing he had managed to break hers into a thousand pieces, smashing it as ruthlessly as he could, the fragments resembling the remnants of a piece of expensive crystal.

Glued back together, it was serviceable but never completely the same.

It only took him seconds to reach her, seconds to throw her world off kilter. "Hello, Cat."

Chapter Three

*A*lainn.

The word filtered through Rory's brain the instant he saw her. It was the Gaelic word for beautiful. Cat was all that and more. The beauty she had possessed seven years ago had been youthful, emerging. Now it was fully realized, shaped and refined by nature into stunning maturity.

Her body, too, had altered. Her curves were fuller, rounder, accentuated by the clinging moss-green sweater set she wore, along with the winter-white, wool trousers. Her hair was longer, flowing past her shoulders and ending midway down her back. If anything, the color was richer, a radiant auburn. A soft fringe of bangs feathered across her forehead, framing her face. When he left, that lovely face had been rounder. It too had subtly modified in the time past. Cheekbones sharper, mouth a fraction softer.

But her eyes, he thought, were still the same. Unchanged in color. Green. The forever green of legend and memories.

It didn't pass Rory's notice that she hadn't said hello in return.

When she finally found her voice, Cat asked, "What brings you here?"

Rory wanted to say *"You."* But the word remained unspoken, trapped in his throat. Instead, he said, "I was in the neighborhood and thought that it might be interesting to indulge myself in a few minutes of nostalgia. To see if anything's changed here."

"Really?" Cat wished that she could believe that's all it was. A simple trip down memory lane; but nothing had ever been simple between them. Not in the long run.

"It appears that you've done quite well for yourself, Cat," Rory murmured, his tone polite. His gaze roamed the expanded shelves, noted the changes and improvements that she'd made to the premises, before returning to her.

"Yes, I have," she responded in the same blandly mild voice, inwardly fighting to maintain her composure. It was a tough battle, what with his whole demeanor screaming *hot and sexy* from the well-remembered black leather jacket he wore open over an expensive-looking oatmeal sweater, dark blue jeans and black boots. From the corner of her eye, Cat caught a twenty-something customer in a Cedar Hill University sweatshirt as she walked nearby give Rory a quick once-over, smiling to herself in silent appreciation.

Suddenly the store seemed smaller, as if it were closing in on Cat. She felt cornered. Trapped by and between the past and the present. And it was all Rory Sullivan's fault. What right did he have to be here as if they'd parted friends? As if their last words had been kind and cordial.

Go away! she screamed silently. *Please, go away. Release me.*

"I'm happy for you, Cat. I know just how much this place meant to you."

She heard the underlying irony in his voice and replied in kind. "It still does."

"That's good. If you put your heart and soul into something it should be worth whatever sacrifice, or effort, you deem necessary to maintain it."

"It is."

Cat sounded so cool and matter-of-fact to him. Almost hard to believe she was the same woman he'd shared numerous hot, sensual hours with, their bodies so close and in tune that it was impossible to tell where one began and the other left off. Her voice had been warm back then, husky with passion; her skin dewed with moisture; her hands as eager to explore as his; her mouth pure excitement and promise.

Clearly that was then, this is now. The woman who stood before him was self-contained, with a "do not disturb" attitude.

Well, what had he expected?

The back-door buzzer rang.

"I'll..." Mary Alice started to say before she was cut off by Cat.

"No," she said, "I'll go." She reached out her hand in a formal manner, praying that it remained steady. "Good to see you again—" she hesitated for the briefest instant, as if forming a little-used foreign phrase "—Rory."

Had she imagined it or had his eyes quickly turned darker, sharper, hotter?

"Likewise, Cat."

With a quicksilver movement, she was gone, and he was left standing alone, Mary Alice off to answer the loudly ringing phone.

Their hands had barely touched before she withdrew hers, as if contact with his skin was abhorrent. Or, could it be, he wondered, that she had felt the same jolt of electricity that he had? Had she been shocked that it still existed? Frightened by the implications? Or appalled?

Rory glanced at the door that led to the back room, a smile tilting the corners of his mouth.

Cat imagined that she could still feel the tingling in her skin upon the contact with his. Handshakes. An everyday occurrence that she never even gave a second thought to.

Until today.

Until now.

Until him.

The brush of flesh against flesh had instantly summoned memories of other times, other caresses: his palms skimming lazily along her breast or thigh, a drift of his lean fingers along her neck or over her arm.

But she'd held on to her jolted emotions. Kept her cool.

Pleased with herself, Cat counted and signed for the shipment, happy that she had maintained her poise in dealing with Rory. Cat could never show him that he still had any influence on her emotions.

"Anything going out?" the UPS man asked, breaking into Cat's thoughts.

"Yes," she answered, retrieving the package that was being sent to a customer. Her back was to the stockroom door, so she didn't see the man who entered behind her.

Rory quietly stepped into the room. While he understood that he had been dismissed by his former lover, he wasn't ready to go. Not yet. Not until he had a chance to talk to Cat some more. He hadn't come all this way to walk away now, not without a fight. Not without trying to get through to her. He still felt the pull, the burning, fire-in-the-gut attraction. If anything, it was stronger than ever. Hotter than before.

His glance fell on her desk, as cluttered as his own, littered with papers, books, various odds and ends. He stepped closer, picking up an item of stationery, one finger tracing the design of an embossed silver harp nestled in a bed of shamrocks on a notecard. Rory smiled. The artist had taken time, producing a fine product. Like Cat's store, it was special, one of a kind, much like the lady herself.

He was just about to announce his presence, ask her if she'd consider coming out with him for a drink, anything to prolong the moment, when his eyes fell on a framed photograph on Cat's desk. Reaching out his hand, he picked it up.

Cat turned around, having locked the back delivery door. She was startled to see Rory standing nearby; then it quickly occurred to her where he was and what he had in his hand. She saw the ready smile fade from his lips, replaced by a dawning comprehension at what he held.

Her feet were rooted to the spot, unable to carry her the few steps across the floor so that she could remove the object from his hand. Cat could only stare at him as he examined the photo. Damn, why hadn't she thought to hide the picture in her desk drawer? Put it away until he was gone.

Because she thought she was safe. It never crossed

her mind that he would follow her in here. Obviously he hadn't taken her goodbye as final.

Rory raised his eyes from the photograph, meeting Cat's across the room. "Who is she?" he asked rhetorically as his heart already knew the answer.

"My daughter," she replied.

His response was immediate, cutting her to the quick. "And mine."

"Yes." Cat couldn't deny the fact, especially since the truth was there to see.

That one word hung suspended in the air between them. It cut through years and memories like the snap of a whip.

Rory's glance fell back to the photo. *His daughter. His child.* His fingers glided over the glass that protected the photo inside, as if he could somehow feel the warmth of the little girl underneath. "Why didn't you tell me?"

"I had my reasons." She couldn't get into this with him here and now.

"Oh, did you?" he asked, his tone cool, shock at this turn of events suddenly invading him like the sharp pricks of a hot needle.

"Yes." Again that single word crackled in the space that separated them.

Moments passed slowly with no words spoken, like thick syrup poured from a cold bottle, the silence broken only by the measured breathing of two people worlds apart.

Finally, the intrusive *brrr*ing of the phone snapped Cat back to reality. While she answered the call, Rory slipped the small framed photograph into his jacket pocket. He waited until Cat put the caller on hold and then said, "We'll talk later."

There was no mistaking the surety of his words, nor

the determined look in his eyes before he left. Moving on autopilot, Cat went about her task, locating the book her customer wanted from a pile of special orders waiting to be called, and then setting it aside, all the while remembering the look in Rory's eyes, the set of his face as he discovered the existence of his child.

Her child.

Their child.

"What's wrong?" Mary Alice asked as soon as she was finished with her customer, following Cat into the back room. "Professor Sullivan walked out of here as if in a trance." Her eyes shifted to the empty space on the desk. "He knows, doesn't he?"

"Knows?"

"That he's Tara's father."

Cat lifted her downcast eyes. "How—"

"Did I guess?" Mary Alice interjected, a knowing smile on her face. "It wasn't all that hard, Cat. Your daughter resembles her father way too much. When you first told me that you were pregnant, I suspected the identity of your baby's father, and when Tara was born, it was there on her face, the feminine version that decorates the dust jackets of his books."

"Can't deny the obvious then, can I?" Cat sank into her comfortable desk chair, idly running one hand through her hair.

"Certainly not the fact that he's one handsome devil." Mary Alice's smile compressed as she asked her next question. "Tara doesn't know, does she?"

"No. And why didn't you ever say anything?"

"Wasn't my place to."

Cat acknowledged her friend's discretion. "Thanks."

"So what are you going to do?"

Cat shrugged her shoulders. "I wish I knew."

"If I can be of any help, you've only got to ask," Mary Alice offered. "I imagine it can't be easy what with him just showing up again after all these years."

"Thanks, but I got myself into this quagmire, so it's my responsibility to get myself out." Cat stood up, taking a few steps before stopping and perching on the stack of boxes the UPS man had brought. "I've been afraid that someday I might have to face this, even though I really didn't think I'd ever see him again. When Rory left, I figured that that was it. I was safe with my secret as long as he remained in Ireland. It never occurred to me that he would ever come back here." She stood up again. "But that was just a dream. An illusion that I chose to believe in."

Cat gave a short snort of laughter. "Well, dreams don't last, and illusions can sometimes become all too real."

"Why didn't you ever tell him about the baby, if you don't mind my asking?"

"Because she was my responsibility. I wanted her."

Mary Alice pointed out, "You didn't create her yourself."

"No, but it was my decision to have her."

"That really doesn't answer my question."

Cat paused a moment before speaking. "It's not an especially original story."

"What is?"

That remark brought a smile to Cat's lips. "Rory didn't want kids."

"He told you that?"

Cat nodded her head. "In no uncertain terms. A few weeks after we started seeing one another, I ran into a college friend with her new baby. We stopped to chat for a few minutes and when she left, I mentioned to Rory that Nancy got what she'd always wanted, a child. I saw that chance meeting as an opening, to see what he thought about having kids. You know how important family is to me.

"Well, that was when he informed me they had no place in his future, in how he saw his life. They demanded too much time, too much energy, energy he could put to better use, he said, getting ahead in the academic world. So you see, a child would have been the last thing Rory would have wanted to know about."

"He might have changed his mind if you had told him."

Cat shook her head. "I doubt it. He wanted no ties, no commitments. Nothing to hold him back from where he was going and what he wanted to do."

"But that was then."

"And this is now," Cat replied. "I know."

"So what'll you do?"

"Go home and think how I can best to tell my daughter that I have a surprise for her."

Rory doffed his black leather jacket upon entering his town house, removing the photo from it beforehand. Walking to the butler's table, he poured himself a stiff whiskey, took a seat and set the photo down where he could see it.

Sipping the potent liquid, Rory contemplated the truth that the picture contained.

A *daughter*. Flesh of his flesh. Blood of his blood. A part of him that he hadn't known about until now. No clue. No inkling. No warning.

Children had never played an important part in his life, nor had he thought they ever might. He had other priorities, other interests in life.

Nice in theory.

But theory had been shot to hell less than an hour ago. Now he was faced with reality in the shape of a dimpled, black-haired little girl who smiled with his face.

And he didn't even know her name.

"Rory knows."

The man Cat addressed her words to hadn't even joined her in the booth of the popular restaurant that catered to the legal crowd in Cedar Hill before she spoke. Bulging briefcases, three-piece suits, beepers and cell phones were *de rigueur* for all the attorneys present. The man who slid his tall, lean frame into the seat opposite her was no exception.

"And what's he going to do about it?"

"How should I know, Brendan?"

"He gave you no hint of what he intends?" His tone was direct and to the point, the same way that he conducted himself in the courtroom.

Cat let out an exasperated sigh. Sometimes her big brother could be so infuriating with his cool, precise legal mind. "I wasn't speaking to you as a client."

"Sorry," he said, extending his hand across the width of the table that separated them, giving hers a squeeze. "Force of habit."

Cat suspected that it was just that, and maybe the influence of that overly cool woman that Brendan lived with. She often wondered how her brother, the warm and open man she knew and loved, managed sharing his life with someone who derived her greatest pleasure from her work, first and foremost. People came a distant second.

"I forgive you, but you know that already, don't you," she said.

Brendan gave her one of his lazy, winning smiles and held up his left hand toward her, fingers folded, thumb extended.

Cat smiled at the familiar gesture and held up hers, pressing it against her brother's in an automatic response. Both carried a small scar from their childhood upon their respective thumbs when they decided to become what they called "double blood" brothers. To the five-and nine-year-old, that was a stronger bond than merely being brother and sister. This sharing and mixing was a sacred trust. It was a promise made and forever kept.

Their moment was interrupted by the arrival of the waitress, who served a mug of hot tea to Cat and a large glass of dark, imported beer to Brendan.

"I warned you that this might happen when he came back."

"I know. It's just that…"

"What?" Brendan probed, his handsome face reflecting his concern for his sister's welfare.

"Rory's changed."

"How?"

"In subtle ways," she explained. "I saw it in his eyes. Heard it in his voice."

Brendan put his half-empty glass back on the table. "Maybe you were seeing what you wanted to see, sis. Underneath," he said with a sharp, revealing tone, "he's probably still the same selfish bastard that took advantage of your trust and your love."

Cat smile at her brother's staunch defense of her, but she couldn't pretend that she had been a helpless victim in her affair with Rory. "I knew what I was doing."

Brendan cocked his head to one side. "Did you? He was your first lover, someone a lot more experienced than you."

Her first lover. Her *only* lover. "Yes. It wasn't really his fault if I misunderstood what he wanted out of the relationship, if I fell in love and he didn't."

"He pursued you," Brendan pointed out, the tactics he used every day in his job as an assistant district attorney slipping through once again. He was making a case, laying out the facts as he saw them.

"Because I wanted him to, Brendan."

He rolled his eyes. "I can't believe that you're defending him."

"I'm not," Cat protested. "I'm merely stating how it was."

"I know how it was," her brother replied, concern for his younger sister evident in his long-lashed, hazel-green eyes. "I saw for myself that it damn near killed you when he walked away from the relationship."

"But I survived."

"Without him," he said sharply.

"Yes, but with a part of him that grew inside me, the best part of him and me."

"And now he wants what exactly? To take up where he left off? To try again to screw up your life?"

"Honestly—" she said "—I don't know." Cat paused, taking another sip of her drink before she continued. How could she know what Rory wanted? It wasn't as if she had a pipeline into his brain, or his heart. Maybe, once. Or so she had flattered herself into thinking.

"Come on, Cat," Brendan insisted. "He must have

given you some indication why he suddenly showed up on your doorstep.''

''Perhaps for old time's sake.''

Brendan made a sound of disbelief.

''Why he came is not the point.''

''Then what is?''

''The reaction I saw on his face when he looked at Tara's picture. A look I'd never seen before.''

''Ego,'' Brendan retorted. ''I've seen far too many cases of that in my work. A shot of sperm doesn't make someone a father. It doesn't automatically endow them with the qualities of a good parent. It takes caring, concern, responsibility and the ability to love. Things we learned growing up. Things Mr. Sullivan lacks.''

''Maybe,'' Cat mused aloud, ignoring her brother's caustic comments, ''it was just shock. Being confronted with a child you didn't know existed, a child you never wanted, must have been disconcerting.''

''That's not your problem,'' Brendan stated. ''If he'd stayed around, thought about you more, about what you wanted and needed instead of just himself…''

''I can't afford to look at the situation like that,'' Cat insisted.

Her brother's eyes narrowed. ''You don't think that he'll try and stake a claim to Tara, do you?''

Cat's answer was soft, barely above a whisper. ''I hope not.''

''Because he'd be in for the fight of his life if he tried. What's one Sullivan against the Kildares?''

Her brother's words played over and over again in Cat's head on the drive home. True, she had a family that loved and supported her. Siblings who would stand by her; a mother and father who weren't afraid to fight for their children's happiness; cousins, aunts and uncles on both sides who believed strongly in the concept of family loyalty.

But Rory had money, she knew. Lots and lots of money. Old money. A sizable trust fund that allowed him to do what he wanted, whenever he wanted.

However, she was getting ahead of herself. He said that he wanted to talk. Understandable. Unnerving, but definitely understandable. Maybe he wanted to be sure that she didn't want something from him. That could be it.

And then again it might not be.

She had to stop torturing herself with worry. She mustn't allow Tara to see her upset. Her daughter came first, last, always.

So how was she going to tell Tara? What magic words could she use? What could she say to explain?

Cat pulled her car into the parking lot of the school, a smile breaking through her dark mood when she saw her daughter.

Tara ran to her mother's car, her pretty face beaming with happiness. "Look at what we got from the computer, Mommy." She handed her mother the printout as soon as she got into the car and received her welcoming hug and kiss, which she reciprocated. "Mrs. Robb talked to us about tracing our roots. Isn't that funny, like we were plants?"

Cat's lips curved in a bittersweet smile, the irony almost overwhelming her. Her daughter, being helped to discover more about her family past. "Was it fun?"

Tara nodded her head. "Yeah. I got to read all about Ireland and where the Kildares came from. I'm gonna call Nanny and Pop and tell them to come over so that they can see it too."

"Not tonight, sweetheart."

"Why?"

"Your nanny is working late at the clinic tonight and your grandfather is out of town with my cousin Dylan at a conference for police detectives, don't you remember?"

Tara nodded. "I forgot."

"That's okay, sweetie. I'm sure that when they can, they'd both love to see what you found." This was the opening she needed, however unexpected, to introduce the subject of her child's father. But should she? What if Rory really wasn't interested at all in his daughter. Would that be giving Tara more information than she needed? More than she was ready for, especially if her father expressed no interest whatsoever in seeing her, meeting her? Would telling Tara that she had a flesh-and-blood father do more harm than good?

Cat wished that she knew. Wished that she had some real clue.

Until she had, she couldn't bring herself to tell Tara that her biological father was in town.

Rory stood outside the modest house, taking note in the fading light of the touches that seemed welcoming. Bright clusters of fall flowers surrounded the brick walkway and continued around the base of the house. Adding a touch of class were numerous rosebushes, some reaching up to cling, the others nestled comfortably. Even from where he stood, the air was redolent with the smell. A hanging bird feeder on a nearby maple tree was still attracting customers to sample its tasty goods.

The house itself had an old feel to it, though he guessed it to be fairly new. It didn't stand there and scream "Notice me" as did many new homes, ostentatious and overdone. Its stone and wood blended into the landscape seamlessly.

Somehow, it seemed right for Cat. Perfect.

Rory climbed the wide stone steps and rang the bell.

Less than a minute later, a porch light flicked on and the oak door, with its stained-glass insert, was opened.

His words were direct, aimed at the woman who stood sentinel. "I'm here to see her."

Chapter Four

Cat stood in the doorway, blocking his entrance into her home. "She doesn't know anything about you, Rory."

One of his black eyebrows arched slightly. "Why am I not surprised?"

She wet her lips. "It wasn't important."

He stepped closer, less than inches from her. "Is that so?" he inquired, his voice low and soft. "Having a father isn't important to a child?"

"Tara doesn't have a father."

"Because I didn't know I had a daughter," Rory retorted.

"Bull."

"What's that supposed to mean?" he demanded. "And, would you mind if I came inside? I'd rather not discuss my—*our* personal business in the street."

"It's hardly the street," Cat responded.

"It's still not private."

"I don't want Tara upset."

"I didn't come here to do that," he stated. "I only want to see her. That isn't really too much to ask, now, is it?"

"I suppose not," she conceded, then stepped aside and let him enter, shutting the door behind him.

Rory was enveloped by the warmth of the interior of her home, a sharp contrast to Cat's cool demeanor. He could smell the subtle scent of applejack as he followed her into a small room off the hall that was dominated by an overstuffed floral couch, topped by a sweater-like white throw.

She pulled the pocket door closed and when she did, Cat felt as if all the air had been locked outside the room, forcing her to take a deep breath before she spoke. "You've got to promise me that you won't say anything to upset Tara," she reiterated. "Or," she stated plainly, "you can turn around and leave."

"That's not my intention, I can assure you." Rory leaned back into the seat of the couch, enjoying the enveloping feel of comfort, like a welcome hug. It was so different from the formal furniture that he was used to growing up in his parents' house, and what he had lived with in Ireland. He threw her a glance, placed his hand on the couch, indicating that she should take a seat next to him.

Cat ignored the invitation and remained standing. Right now, sitting so close to him, would be a mistake; it would be too cozy, too intimate, something she couldn't afford. Instead, she kept the focus where it belonged—on what he was doing there. "And what are your intentions?" she demanded.

"Just to meet her, for now."

"For now?" she repeated, her tone skeptical.

He quickly rose from the couch, coming closer. "Cat, you can't expect me to know what I'll feel or how I'll react."

"She's a child, Rory, and you're a stranger."

"Through no fault of my own."

Cat was stung by his words. "Can you honestly tell me that you would have been thrilled if I'd told you that I was pregnant? 'Children have no place in my life,'" she said, repeating the very words he'd said to her.

She waited for a moment. "What? No snappy comeback? No denial?"

"I remember what I said," he admitted. "But I can't walk away now that I know."

"Can't you?"

"No."

It wasn't so much the word as the tone he used when uttering that one word that convinced Cat that he was serious. "Okay."

"Then I can see her?"

She searched his eyes. "Yes. But only for a few minutes."

"That's all?"

"For now." She turned his words back on him. "Wait here."

After she left, Rory walked a few paces to the fireplace, stared at the collection of photos on the carved mantel. There was a silver-framed photo of Cat and her folks, taken, he guessed, when she was in college; another of her brother and sister, who looked older than he remembered, so that it must have been taken recently; a third that included everyone, with Tara as the focal point. There was a Christmas tree in the background, heavily weighted with ornaments and lights. The little

girl in the picture looked happy beyond belief, surrounded by a tight-knit clan that obviously adored her.

"Rory."

He spun around and the breath caught in his throat.
Holding her mother's hand was his secret child.

"Tara, I'd like you to meet Professor Sullivan, someone Mommy knew a long time ago." Cat couldn't pretend and say "an old friend." That would have been a
joke considering their past.

The little girl released her mother's hand and stepped
forward, extending her own, as she had been taught.
"Hello."

Rory bent down so that the child wouldn't have to
crane her neck upward. "Hello, Tara," he said, taking
her tiny hand in his. It was warm and smooth, soft as
down. Her dark blue eyes were replicas of his own.

"You sound funny."

"Tara," Cat admonished.

"But he does," the little girl protested.

"I expect that's because I haven't lived in America
for a while."

"Where were you?"

"A faraway place called Ireland."

Her face beamed. "Oh, I know where that is."

"You do?"

She nodded her head. "Across the Atlantic, miles and
miles from here."

He smiled at her description of distance. "That's
right."

"I'm Irish," the little girl stated.

"We have that in common then. So am I," Rory said,
oddly fascinated by the little girl.

"I'm a Kildare."

He kept his eyes on Tara though he was tempted to shoot a look to Cat. "Are you now?"

"Uh-huh. Wanna see my ring?"

"Sure."

Tara stuck out her other hand, proudly showing off a gold Claddagh ring. "Isn't it pretty? My uncle Brendan got it for me last Christmas."

"Very pretty indeed, sweetheart."

"He took me to the circus when it was in Philadelphia."

Rory reached out his hand and gently touched the little girl's face. "He must love you very much."

Cat answered. "He does."

It was easy to see why, he thought. The little girl seemed both bright and sweet.

"Say good-night to Mr. Sullivan, Tara. You've got some homework to do, then it's off to bed."

"Goodbye, Mr. Sullivan."

"And what else?" Cat prompted, pleased that Rory had kept his word not to upset their daughter.

"It was very nice to meet you," Tara said.

Rory's reply was genuine and heartfelt. "It was my pleasure to finally meet you, Tara."

"Are you gonna come back and see us again?"

Rory glanced up at Cat and then back to Tara. "Would you like that?"

"Do you tell stories?"

"I've been known to on occasion."

"My grandpop tells stories. Really good ones."

"Then I'll tell you a story the next time I come, okay?"

Tara's eyes widened. "What about?"

Rory smiled. "An Irish princess named Tara and a magic spell."

"That's my name."

"Indeed, and a grand one it is, sweetheart."

"It's a special place in Ireland," she confided.

"I know. I've been there."

"Really?"

"Truly."

"Someday I'll go there," she said with all the certainty of a child.

"As well you should."

Cat put one hand on her daughter's shoulder. "Tara, stop dawdling. Say goodbye and go on upstairs. I'll be there in a few minutes."

"Bye," the child said as she bolted from the room, leaving the two adults alone.

Rory stood up, easing the ache in his legs from crouching so long. "When can I see her again?"

"Are you sure that you want to?"

"I've never been more sure of anything in my life," he said.

Cat hesitated, not knowing what to make of his request. "I don't know."

"She's my daughter, too, Cat. Fair is fair."

"All right," she conceded, acknowledging his point. "But I'm doing this for Tara, you understand?"

"Loud and clear, Miss Kildare."

"What about Saturday night? Dinner?" As soon as the words had left her mouth she wanted to recall them. What had ever possessed her to ask him to come for a meal?

He accepted her invitation before she could change her mind. "I'd like that, thanks."

She escorted him to the door, still wondering why she had asked him to dinner. Sharing a meal would dredge up painful memories, not to mention scratch old wounds. However, for Tara's sake, she would do it.

"Would you like me to bring anything?"

"That won't be necessary."

"But I'd like to."

"Then dessert would be nice."

"Anything in particular?" She used to love chocolate, he recalled, in any shape or form.

"Whatever you'd like. Doesn't matter."

"Thanks for letting me see her."

"You're welcome."

"We still have to talk, Cat."

"Some other time."

"Just so you know. I won't be put off forever."

"Is that a warning?" she asked.

"No," he said silkily. "A promise."

"Good*bye,* Rory."

"Good *night,* Cat."

She stood there, watching him walk away, her eyes intent on his retreating figure. Unlike before, she knew he would be back. As his car sped away, she closed the door and breathed a deep sigh. Just being in the same room with him was difficult. That old attraction was still there. As strong as before. Yet tempered. It had to be. Now there was Tara to think about.

Speaking of her daughter, Cat hurried up the stairs and into Tara's bedroom, where she found the little girl curled up in her bed, storybook in her lap.

"Sorry that I'm late, honey, but I had to see our guest out," she said as she settled herself next to Tara in the antique maple bed. A flea-market find, she bought it last year and removed the layers of white paint, restoring the treasure below to her daughter's delight.

"He's a nice man, Mommy."

She pulled her daughter into her arms, hugging her. "You think so?"

"Uh-huh."

"Why?"

The little girl shrugged. "I like his voice."

"Even though you said that it was 'funny'?"

Tara laughed. "It's a nice kind of funny."

Cat smoothed back the hair from Tara's face. Did her child somehow feel a connection to Rory? A connection that had nothing to do with reason and everything to do with blood. Or was it simply Tara's outgoing personality at work? The easy charm that she'd inherited from her father?

"So, you wouldn't mind if he came to dinner then?"

"When?" the child asked eagerly. "Tomorrow?"

"No, Saturday."

"Can we have pizza?"

That item was currently Tara's favorite, along with chocolate milk shakes. "If you'd like."

Tara nodded her head. "Goody."

"Then pizza it is."

Rory needed a shower. Preferably cool to take the edge off his heated nerves. Something to erase the warmth of memories that threatened to overwhelm him.

He walked into his bathroom, pulled open the glass door of the shower stall and turned on the taps, full blast. Removing his tailored boxers, Rory stepped inside, letting the water sluice over his body. He closed his eyes and bowed his head, the chill instantly bringing a reaction from his flesh.

Then he thought he felt something. A flicker of sensation, like a finger stroking his back, along his spine. Then lower. Moving slowly and softly.

He'd know that touch anywhere. Cat.

Relaxing, he leaned against the tile, letting the water work its magic, mixing reality and fantasy. Stopping time and then sending it hurtling back, back to when fantasy had been reality....

"Come on. Try it," he coaxed.

Her face was gently tinged with a flush of color. "I'm really not sure."

He held out his hand, inviting her. "What have you got to lose?"

With that challenge thrown down, Cat took it up, joining her lover in the shower. Slippery, slick, his skin felt warm to the touch as she smoothed the soapy washcloth across his back, around the deceptively wide shoulders, down one arm and then the next, all the while enjoying the feel of his taut flesh. Who knew there could be so much pleasure found in getting clean? What was once perfunctory had become pleasurable.

"Turn around," she whispered, her voice husky. Now it was her turn to take the lead.

Rory eagerly did as he was bid, moving carefully in the luxurious space of the glass shower. A wide skylight bathed the room with natural light.

Her hands moved on him again, gently smoothing a path across his chest, through the whorls of dark hair that led her eyes downward. Soon her hands followed, instinct taking over, passion guiding her.

She stole his breath with her intimate kiss, plunging him into a higher and higher plateau of pleasure. Her pure passion ignited a deeper and darker flame in his soul, burning its way into his very marrow.

As no one before.

As no one else since....

Rory's head snapped back as he pushed his hand

through the wet strands of his hair, relishing the intense flashback of the vibrantly sensual moments they'd shared.

Damn! It promised to be a long night.

"You've been very quiet all day," Mary Alice said to Cat as they prepared to close the store.

Cat looked up from counting the cash drawer. "Have I?"

"Yes. It's him, isn't it?"

Him. There didn't have to be a name; she knew. "He's part of it."

"The biggest part, right?"

Cat handed her assistant the money and checks she'd finished with, along with the bank slip. "He came to the house last night."

Mary Alice slipped the day's receipts into a deposit bag and zipped it shut, removing the key from the lock. "And how did that go?"

Cat cleaned up around the cashwrap, dusting the fixture, checking the displays. "I really don't know."

"What do you mean?"

"He said that he came to see Tara."

"Did he?"

Cat understood what her assistant was too polite to ask—*Did you let him?* "Yes. She liked him."

"Does that bother you?"

Cat shrugged her shoulders. "I can't honestly say." She stopped what she was doing, then leaned against the counter.

"Come on, Cat," the older woman insisted. "You've gotta have some opinion. Some inkling of how you feel."

"What if he's changed his mind?" Cat added apprehensively.

"Regarding children?"

Cat nodded.

"Then you'll deal with it the best way you know how."

'I'm not so sure about that.''

"I am."

A small smile curved Cat's mouth. "Thanks for the vote of confidence."

"It's the simple truth."

Cat glanced away. "When has the truth ever been simple for me?"

"You love your daughter," Mary Alice stated. "That's the truth, and you'll do what's best for her."

"What if I don't know what's best for her now?" she asked, turning back to her friend.

"Cat, you've got to stop beating yourself up about this. Who knows? Professor Sullivan may decide being a father really isn't what he wants. Or what he needs. But I do know one thing," her assistant announced.

"And that is?"

"He still wants you."

"What?"

'Big time,'' Mary Alice insisted. "I saw it on his face when he was here."

Maybe he did once, but that was over between them, Cat rationalized later as she drove the short distance to her house. Over and done with. Buried. Both had moved on with their lives.

Or so she'd thought.

Then why had her sleep last night been filled with images of her past with Rory? Images that warmed. Images both bitter and sweet. That first cup of coffee together the morning after they'd first made love. Waking to find Rory carrying a wooden tray into the bedroom, laden with two oversize coffee containers and a fancy box filled with assorted doughnuts. ''Breakfast of champions,'' he laughingly said as he placed the tray over her lap and doffed his clothes, joining her in the snug bed.

She'd opened the taped lid to discover her two favorite kinds inside—vanilla cream-filled and chocolate-covered. ''You're a god,'' she teased, biting into the cream-filled first, the powder dusting her lips.

His mouth served as her napkin, removing all the evidence of her pleasure.

'I'd rather be an Irish king, if you please,'' he retorted, ''with you as my consort.''

Boldly, she replied. ''Then as your queen, I demand satisfaction.''

Rory laughed, his rich baritone ringing out in the silence of the room. ''Which, my lady, I am most happy to provide.'' Gently, he removed the half-eaten doughnut from her hand.

''What are you doing?'' she squealed in delight as he touched the remaining creamy inner filling to her chin, to her neck, then lower.

''You'll see,'' he said, a wicked gleam in his eyes. ''Or better yet, you'll feel.''

His tongue lapped the sweet, white filling from her chin, then moved on to her neck, several heated strokes making the cream disappear. Then, he lowered his head, licking what remained from her taut nipples.

Cat rolled her head from side to side, reveling in the pleasure he was creating, her breath coming in heated gasps.

''Open your mouth, Cat,'' he said softly, then Rory used his tongue again, to scoop out the rest of the filling from the almost empty shell of the doughnut. Then he kissed her, letting her taste it from his mouth.

She'd never eaten another vanilla cream-filled doughnut again after he left. Now if she stopped at the local bakery, it was for muffins, pies or cakes. Never doughnuts.

He'd spent quite a few hours in the children's department of the large chain bookstore. He wanted to get his daughter something special to mark the occasion of his having dinner with Tara and her mother. Having been forced to ask for help, as buying books for children wasn't something he'd ever done before, Rory arrived home with a fair number. Sifting through the stack, he picked one that he thought she would like.

But what did he know?

Tara could hate it.

Or him.

And what if she did. What then?

Damned if he knew. It was all so new, all so strange. To discover he had a part of himself living in another form. A part of Cat. Created by them. Solely and exclusively. Calmly stating you didn't want or need children to make your life complete was one thing. Finding out, *fait accompli,* that you had one was another. When he had originally told Cat, he really had meant it. Believed it.

Things were different now.

While he was looking for the perfect book, he'd taken the opportunity to observe several parents with their kids. Watched as they shopped for and with them. What they chose. How they handled certain situations, trying to imagine himself in their place.

A daddy. A father. Responsible for another human being. Guiding. Nurturing. Protecting. Loving.

Could he?

Even if he could, did he really want to?

And what would Cat have to say if he did? How would she feel? There was no ignoring the fact that she and her child were a package deal. He could possibly have the daughter without the mother, but never the mother without the child.

Tonight was crucial. He hoped that he would discover if all this was just a novelty or if he truly wanted a family. That he still wanted Cat was a given. But he had to sort out his feelings about the little girl.

Tara. A special name for a special child. Special because she was Cat's. Carried in her womb and obviously raised with love.

Did he really have room in his heart for her as well? Could he be the father she would need and love, from now on?

In all honesty, Rory had to admit to himself, he didn't know. But he had to find out. And soon.

Chapter Five

"When's he gonna get here?"

"When's *who* going to get here?" Cat's mother asked as she walked into her daughter's kitchen from the back door, then stopped to hug her granddaughter.

Cat stopped what she was doing, which was setting the table for dinner.

Her mother's sharp green-eyed glance fell to the three places that were set.

"Tara, why don't you go upstairs and play on the computer for a while, honey, since our guest will be here in about an hour."

"Okay," she said, dashing out the door and up the stairs.

"I got your messages, but I didn't have a chance to get back to you," her mother said, helping herself to a cup of freshly brewed coffee. Adding just a dash of sugar, Mary Kildare drank a hearty amount before she repeated her question. "Who's coming to dinner?"

"Rory."

Mary set the cup down on the counter and stared at her child. "Rory, as in Rory Sullivan?"

Cat nodded her head.

Mary took another sip of her coffee. "How did this come about?"

"That's what I was calling to tell you and Dad, except I didn't want to just leave a 'guess what' message on the machine, nor did I want to phone you earlier and disturb your vacation with Aunt Pat. You so rarely have a chance to see your sister since she remarried and moved to Australia. It's hard enough for you to get time away from your patients as it is. Then, when you got home, I knew you'd be busy catching up at the clinic for a few days, and Dad had to go to that conference almost right away."

Mary gave her daughter a sharp look, her eyes reflecting her concern. "News like this was, is—" she stressed "—too important to keep. When did he get back?"

"About a week or so ago."

Her mother glanced at the polished table, a wave of her hand indicating the casual, yet well-appointed setup. She recognized the china, part of a group that Cat had purchased at a recent tag sale. The napkins, fine Irish linen, monogrammed with a distinctive *K,* were part of a set Cat had received from her grandmother when she was twenty-one. "And what's this all about?"

"Tara."

"Has he come to claim her?"

Cat refilled her own mug, pouring a liberal amount of half-and-half into her cup. "He's coming for a meal, that's all." She took a sip. "At least that's all I hope he's come for right now."

"After all these years, to suddenly turn up?" Mary Kildare mused. "How odd."

"He was offered a job at the university, heading up his own department."

"Was he now? And what's that got to do with you and your daughter?"

"Nothing," Cat responded. "And everything. He found out about Tara, and now he wants to get to know her. Or so he said the other day."

"Good," Mary pronounced. "Better late than never."

Cat was surprised. She half expected her mother to have the same attitude as her brother, Brendan, had expressed. "That's not a problem for you?"

"Darling," her mother answered, "it doesn't have a thing to do with me, directly. All that I'm concerned about is how it affects you and my granddaughter. How are you with the situation?"

"Actually, better than I thought," Cat acknowledged, glancing at the clock on the wall. "I'm doing this for Tara, Mom. If there's a chance that she can have a relationship with her father, then I can't deny her that, much as I might have wished he'd never resurfaced. As long as it's to her benefit."

Mary's voice softened. "And what about you?"

"I'll handle it."

"Of course you will," Mary stated unequivocally. "None of my children are quitters, or heaven forbid, whiners. But still, it must have been hard to see him again after all this time."

"It wasn't easy," Cat admitted. Her mother knew especially how hard it had been for her without a father for her child and a lover for her heart. After Brendan and her sister, Kelly, Mary was the first person she'd told about her pregnancy. Mary had been with her in the delivery room as she screamed Rory's name when she gave birth to his daughter. Mary had been there with her when Tara had fallen off a pony when she was three, breaking her wrist and sustaining a concussion. She had agonized with Cat as they waited to find out if Tara would be fine.

"But then," Cat said, returning to what her mother had asked, "I didn't really expect that it would be."

"So you've invited him to dinner. To accomplish what?"

"Maybe alleviate some of my guilt."

Her mother looked skeptical. "What guilt would that be?"

"That I never told him earlier about Tara."

"He didn't want to know."

"That's what I thought. But, seeing them together the other night, I wondered if I did what was right."

'What's done is done, my dear," Mary said gently. "No use trying to recapture what could have been if you'd done something different. It's over. Best to get on with life."

Cat put down her mug and crossed the few feet that separated her from her mother, drawing the older woman into an embrace. "Thank you." She needed her mother's words. Needed to hear that loving acceptance in her voice.

"You don't have to thank me, darling," her mother responded. "I love you."

Cat managed a small smile. "I know. And knowing that helps me more than you can imagine, Mom. Mary Alice even said the same thing to me."

"Then maybe you'd best believe it."

The short silence in the room was broken by the beep of a pager.

Mary Kildare reached for the device that was always with her. She checked the number and laughed softly. "Duty calls." She picked up her daughter's phone and punched in a series of numbers. "Yes. When?"

Cat recognized the focused look in her mother's green eyes as she talked calmly and quickly. She was the consummate professional, able to switch gears in a heartbeat.

"I'm on my way." Mary checked her watch. "In about ten minutes. Goodbye."

"Sorry," she explained. "I've got to run."

This was nothing new to Cat, who'd grown up with her mother's career. "I understand."

Mary hugged her daughter. "Give me a call later, and let me know what happens. Even if it's late."

"All right," Cat said, then asked a favor as she walked her mother to the door. "Will you tell Daddy?"

"Do you want me to?"

"I'd really appreciate it. Of course, he could have already been told by Brendan."

"I doubt that, or he would have said something to me straightaway. We've never kept news concerning our children from one another." She smiled and gave Cat another quick hug, their matching eyes locked. "At least not for long. Give Tara my love."

"Always."

"Don't forget," Mary insisted. "Call me."

"I promise."

Mary walked out the back door and saw the lights from another car as the driver pulled into the driveway and shut the engine off. Unlocking her door with a snap to her key ring, she watched cautiously as the person approached her. The outside sconce lights on the porch were on so that she could see his face clearly when he got closer.

Rory recognized the woman and hid his shock. His former lover's mother was the last person he expected to see tonight. She and Cat shared more than a passing resemblance, which had only strengthened over the years.

He acknowledged her presence with a brief, "Dr. Kildare."

She did likewise, though her greeting was more personal in tone. "Rory." She extended her hand. "How very *interesting* to see you."

He flashed her a charming smile. "Yes, it has been rather a long time, hasn't it?"

"Too long," she answered, and opened her car door. "Sorry that I can't talk, but I have an emergency."

Rory watched her leave, her car quickly departing down the tree-lined street. She hadn't seemed surprised to see him, so Cat must have told her mother that he was coming tonight. And her greeting was pleasant. More so than he would have thought given the circumstances.

He'd always liked Cat's family, even if they had seemed a bit overwhelming at times. Used as he was to a more sedate experience, the boisterous Kildare clan was foreign to him. They thought nothing of challenging each other to any sport, game or intellectual pursuit. They played to win. They also never hesitated to voice an opinion, no matter what the topic. Were constantly wrapped up in each other's lives and proud of it. To them, family was a bond, an unbreakable hold on each other. Solid. Lasting a lifetime.

He recalled Cat's father, a tough cop who'd risen in

the ranks to detective, once saying at a dinner party, over a large glass of Guinness, ''Once a Kildare, forever a Kildare.''

On a whim, he'd once checked out their family motto: *For Honor and Family.*

He didn't know about the former, but the latter certainly fit them perfectly.

And here he was, the errant prodigal contemplating an entrance into this particular pride of lions once again.

Perhaps he was crazy.

Or *lovestruck.* Now there was a nice, poetic term.

Rory glanced up to the darkening sky, observing the full moon in all its glory.

Moonstruck. Falling under a magical spell of enchantment.

He laughed softly. Better get inside, he thought, before he slipped into maudlin sentimentality, ruining the evening before it started.

Cat heard the soft chime of the front doorbell and went to answer it, followed by the fast footsteps of her daughter running down the stairs.

''He's here,'' Tara announced excitedly, reaching for the handle.

''Mind your manners, young lady,'' Cat instructed.

''I will,'' the little girl promised solemnly, stepping back to allow her mother access to the door first.

''Give me your hand, and let's greet our guest.'' Cat unlocked the door and swung it open. ''Welcome.''

She couldn't help but notice the two shopping bags that Rory had with him as he entered the hallway, nor the relaxed way he was dressed. A brown tweed jacket over matching corduroy slacks, topped by a pale gray sweater. He would certainly, in her humble opinion, put any male model who graced the covers of a fashion magazine to shame. He was the real deal.

Rory set the shopping bags down. One carried the label of a chain bookstore. The other, smaller one was from Cedar Hill's best bakery.

"What's in them?" Tara asked, bending over to peer inside both bags.

Rory doffed his jacket and hung it on the nearby hall tree, picking up the larger bag and handing it to Tara. "This is for you," he said with a roguish smile.

"For me?" she asked, unable to hide the enthusiasm from her voice.

"That's right."

Cat watched as her daughter rifled through the bag, pulling out the contents and stacking them on the floor. She met his eyes over her daughter's head. "You didn't have to, Rory."

"I wanted to," he admitted. He picked up the second bag, handing it to Cat. "For dessert."

"What is it?"

"Open it and see."

"Can I open mine now, Mommy?"

Cat looked at the growing pile at her daughter's feet. "How many are there?"

"Just a few things I thought she'd like," Rory replied.

Cat shot him an "are-you-kidding?" glance. "Looks like more than a few."

He shrugged, drawing her attention to the width of his shoulders. She remembered cuddling up against them, the solid warmth they had offered.

"You don't have to bribe her, Rory," Cat said softly so that only he could hear, forcing her mind away from things she didn't want to recall. "She likes you already."

"It wasn't meant as a bribe, Cat," he explained. "Merely a gift. No strings."

Tara ran into the library, her arms full of the presents, jumped up on the couch and tore into them, ripping through the brightly wrapped paper, exposing the book underneath with glee.

At least he had the sense to bring their child books instead of toys, Cat thought as she stepped into the room, Rory close by her side. Tara loved to read, a trait obviously inherited from both sides of her genes. The many bookcases in Cat's compact house attested to that fact.

She gave a quick look at Rory's choices, mentally approving of what he'd selected.

His voice whispered from behind her. "Aren't you going to open the dessert?"

"Sure." Cat saw that Tara was quite content to examine each and every book that her father had given her. "Would you like some coffee?" she asked, leaving her daughter to examine her new treasures.

"I'd love some," he replied, following her down the hallway to the kitchen.

Rory watched as she moved gracefully about the room, removing a mug from the cabinet. That she remembered exactly how he took it flattered him.

And speaking of flattering—he couldn't help but notice how the jeans that she wore flattered her. A soft, buff shade, they hugged her rounded hips and long legs, accentuating her very female curves. With them, she wore a pale green, long-sleeved shirt, tucked in, all the buttons fastened.

Two fantasy scenarios played out in his head. In the first, he unbuttoned the shirt slowly, revealing her flesh one bit of skin at a time, dotted each inch with languid kisses. The second, more heated, was that he ripped the green silk open, scattering the pearlized buttons across the hardwood floor, the sound of them falling drowned out by the fervent cries of ecstasy that escaped her lips as he tasted her, leaving a scorched-earth trail in his wake.

Blissfully unaware of her guest's thoughts, Cat handed him the mug, careful not to let their hands touch.

"Thank you."

"No problem," she responded, focusing her attention on the bag with the dessert. She pulled out the distinctive box inside, setting it down on the counter. For an instant, she wanted to mimic her daughter and simply rip open the lid and see what was inside. However, she pushed aside that instinct, opting for maturity.

"Aren't you going to open it now?" Rory asked as Cat moved to put the box into the refrigerator.

"Should I?"

"You'll be sorry if you don't," he said softly.

Why was he wearing that captivatingly smug smile? she wondered as she slit the tape that was holding the white sides of the box together. She glanced at the oven, wondering if she had turned it on way too high, as it suddenly felt overly warm in the room. Or was it from the heat she thought she saw in his eyes?

Her soft gasp of surprise echoed in the kitchen as she lifted her eyes from the contents to him and back again.

"I thought you'd be pleased."

It was more than that, she thought as she lifted the cake out and set it on the counter. This was a work of art. It raised dessert to a new level.

Dark, dark chocolate covered the round layer cake, topped by a semicircle of white icing roses on one side; the other was draped with a frosting spray of wisteria, the purple flowers cascading down the side and around the bottom. It was one of her favorite flowers, ever since she first saw them during a trip to England when she was in college.

Funny that after all these years, he still remembered.

"I've never seen anything like this."

"I hope not," he said with a laugh.

"It's far too exquisite to eat."

"Yet that's its purpose."

" I know," she insisted, "but it still seems a shame to desecrate the work."

"It's meant to be enjoyed, Cat," he said, his words flowing over her suggestively. "Savored. Shared."

She parted her lips and wet them with her tongue, causing an instantaneous reaction on his part. Blood pounded hotly in his veins, pooled deep in his groin. He wanted to kiss her. Take her lips with his and sample them without reservation, for hours on end. Remove that prim shirt and explore the skin beneath. Fold her body into his, feel and taste the curves, each and every one.

But he couldn't.

At the look in his eyes, Mary Alice's words came back to haunt Cat. *He still wants you.* Let's not go there, she told herself. "I'd better put this away."

"Good idea. Some things are better when you have to wait for them. Makes the ultimate fulfillment all the richer, don't you agree?"

Did she detect another meaning to his words? "Anticipation spices the outcome," she countered. "For some things, yes."

"Others you want right away," he continued, "the hunger is so great. The need is immediate and must be satisfied then and there, damn the consequences."

"Instant gratification." Why couldn't she shake the image that suddenly formed in her head? Him and her, tearing off their clothes, surrendering to the hot, pulsing need of desire, right there on the hardwood floor. So intense, so passionate a union that they didn't even take the time to remove all their clothes. Quick and fast, without preliminaries. Primal and atavistic. Elemental as a raging storm.

God, what was wrong with her?

It was him. His influence. Triggering old feelings, old wants, like a Pavlovian experiment.

"Do you like pizza?" That, she figured, was a much safer area to explore.

At her prosaic question, Rory blinked. He could have sworn that Cat felt the heat between them the same as him. Why else could he see the look in her eyes, as if she was experiencing pleasure? He could see the flush of color in her cheeks, the glimmer of awareness.

Cat wanted to ignore it. Pretend that it, this ever-present chemistry didn't exist. But she couldn't. Any more than he could.

Not as long as either one of them was alive.

"Yes," he replied.

"Good. It's Tara's choice for tonight. So what would you like on yours? I've got a selection," she said, putting the cake on a raised and covered plate into the fridge and pulling out a tray laden with toppings.

"You're making it yourself?"

'That's part of the fun."

"What does Tara like?"

"Her current favorite is white, topped with chicken and extra cheese."

Rory laughed. Easy to see that his daughter was a little lady with a mind of her own. A trait she inherited from both her parents. "Eclectic."

"Very." Cat also removed the pizza shells, fixing a small one for Tara.

"I like sausage and pepperoni, extra cheese."

"So do I."

"I remember," he said. Very clearly. They'd shared a large pizza once, for dinner at his old apartment, each sampling the other's slice as she introduced him to her favorite singer, Bruce Springsteen. It had tasted even better heated up the next morning, eaten in bed, listening to the Boss.

She worked efficiently, keeping her eyes on what she was preparing, all the while conscious of him in the room, less than a foot from her. He wore a different cologne tonight than she remembered. This was a spicier scent, a bold blend that complemented his masculinity.

She sliced a glance in his direction, caught him looking at her. Immediately, she refocused on what she was doing.

"Do I make you nervous?"

"Hardly," she replied, shoving the pizzas into the oven and setting the timer. "A man in my house, my kitchen, my *anywhere* is not a novelty." She let him think of that what he would. Only she knew that since him no one had been in her bed. That wasn't his business. Especially since she doubted that he could make the same claim regarding a woman.

How many had there been? Had he loved any of them?

Who cared if he had? That fact wasn't her business either. Idle speculation wasn't conducive to lightening up her mood.

"Really?" he drawled. Who? When? How many? Damned if he didn't want to ask. Damned if he couldn't stand knowing.

She turned around and faced him. "It was very sweet of you to bring the books for Tara. She'll make good use of them."

"I'm glad." He stepped closer. "I didn't know what else would be appropriate, given her age, and the fact that I don't really know much about her. Then it occurred to me—a child of ours was sure to be a reader."

A child of ours.

"A very good guess considering our respective backgrounds."

"I thought so," he admitted. "A lot easier than trying to pick out a toy or doll."

The picture of Rory wandering the aisles of the local toy stores brought a smile to Cat's lips. He'd be a fish out of water.

"What's so funny?" He hadn't missed the mirth that she was trying to hold back. Her eyes sparkled. Her mouth twitched.

"The thought of you pushing a shopping cart up and down the aisles of the Toy Palace. It's a hoot."

One eyebrow raised. "A hoot?"

"Funny," she explained.

"Oh."

"You must admit, it's not your field of expertise."

His tone was rueful. "Obviously."

"Truthfully, it wasn't mine either. But I learned."

"So can I."

"If you want to," she answered, hoping he would reveal his plans.

At that moment Tara interrupted them. "These books are really wonderful, Mommy," she exclaimed.

"You like them, then?"

She nodded her head.

"Then what do you say?"

Tara stood before Rory, gazing up at the tall stranger. "Thank you very much."

"You're quite welcome."

"Would you like to see my others?"

He glanced toward Cat. "If your mother has no objections."

"Go ahead. I have a few things to take care of here."

Tara held out her hand and Rory enfolded it in his much larger one. "Let's go," she said, pulling him along.

Cat expelled the breath she was holding, relaxed the hands that had suddenly clenched. She shouldn't feel threatened. Logically she understood that. But logic was different from the heart. She wanted to be there with them, monitor what was being said.

However, she held back, giving them a chance. A few minutes alone cost her nothing but a few moments of uncertainty that she was doing the right thing for her daughter. Her instinct told her to hold her child tight, form a protective barrier around her.

She couldn't. Life intruded whether one wanted it to or not. There was no getting around that.

Rory stood in his daughter's bedroom as she proudly showed off her collection of books. Two bookcases of different sizes stood against one wall. On top of the smaller one was a brightly decorated pail.

"Wanna see my shells?" Without waiting for his answer, Tara walked over and grabbed the pail, giving it to Rory. "I got lots of them."

He examined the shore scenes on the outside of the metal container, then glanced at the numerous shells of all shapes and sizes inside.

"Aren't they neat?" She stuck her hand in and pulled out a larger one. "This is an oyster shell. Isn't it pretty?"

"Very lovely."

"And see this one?" Tara asked, pulling out another shell. "It's from a crab. We got it at the shore in August." She ran to the bookcase, selecting a large paperback book. "There's lots of pictures of shells in here."

Rory bent down and flipped through, sharing the book with the little girl, who oohed and aahed over her favorites.

"Do you like the beach?" he asked her.

"Uh-huh," Tara answered, picking out another shell to show to Rory. "We had a big house on the sand this summer."

"Just you and your mom?" Rory felt a slight hesitation in using the little girl to get information, yet he had to know if Cat was there with another man.

"No. There were lots of people. My nan and pop, Aunt Kelly, some of my cousins."

Tara's enthusiasm was a contrast to the only memory he had of visiting the shore as a child. His parents had taken him when he was about eight. It was an exclusive resort, filled with the required staff, the best that money could provide. He was given everything, everything but fun and freedom. How much different it might have been had he had other family there, or friends to play with.

"That sounds wonderful."

"It was, especially when my mommy and Aunt Kelly took us to the fair. We went on the rides and ate cotton candy and met some clowns."

She was a happy, well-adjusted little girl, he thought, who seemed to have a good life, even if she lacked a father. Cat had done a wonderful job with their daughter, molding and shaping Tara into someone very special.

"Do you have any children?" Tara asked.

It was how Cat found them when she came upstairs. She heard her daughter ask that question and froze, waiting to see how Rory would respond.

He never expected that question would hurt. "If I did, I think that I'd like her to be just like you."

Tara giggled. "Really?"

"Oh yes," he said, reaching out his hand and touching the little girl's head, the hair soft and dark, so like his own. Unexpectedly, his voice choked somewhat. "Just like you."

"Dinner's ready," Cat stated, rescuing the situation before it turned stickier.

"We're having pizza tonight," Tara spoke up as she collected her pail and returned it to its place on the bookcase.

Rory quickly glanced at Cat before resuming watching Tara. "Your favorite."

"How did you know?" the child asked.

"Your mommy told me."

Tara considered that, then asked, "What do you like to eat?"

"I'm partial to fish."

The little girl threw her mother a glance. "What's partial?"

Rory responded first. "It means that I *like* fish, the same way you do pizza."

"Then I want to try fish next, Mommy. The same kind he likes."

"We'll see."

Tara wasn't dropping the topic. "And Mr. Sullivan can help us eat it, okay?"

Rory's lips tilted upward in a smile. He addressed his question to Tara. "Am I being invited back?"

She shook her head yes, then sheepishly looked toward her mother. "Can he?"

"If you'd like that."

"Then let it be my treat," he suggested.

"I didn't know you cooked," Cat said.

"I don't," he admitted with a careless shrug. "However, I do know how to select a restaurant, use a microwave, or have something catered. So, will you let me take you two lovely ladies—" Cat could hear the hint of a lilt in his voice as he pressed on the charm "—to dinner?"

"Can we, Mommy?" Tara asked, excited.

She carefully thought it over for a moment before yielding to the offer. "All right." Cat wet her lips, and her eyes met Rory's. "Now," she said, holding out her hand for her daughter's, "let's eat."

Chapter Six

"I can't believe that it's been two weeks already," Cat declared as she and Mary Alice shared a cup of morning coffee in the back room prior to opening the store one morning.

"Are you seeing him regularly?"

Cat shrugged, casually flipping through a publisher's catalog. "Pretty much. As often as our schedules permit, so he can get to know his daughter better."

"What's Tara think of him?"

Cat gave her assistant a rueful smile. "That he's wonderful. Rory tells her stories and tries to spoil her, as much as I will allow."

"Sounds like they're getting along very well."

"Yes. She's become quite fond of him. More so every day."

"I take it that the feeling's mutual?"

"I think so. I've watched him with her. Little by little, he's accepting her as his daughter."

"And are you accepting she has a father?" Mary Alice asked as she bit into a blueberry muffin. "Not just a biological statistic, but as a real father?"

Cat poured herself a refill and added some to her assistant's cup as well. "I'm certainly trying to."

"Really?"

"For Tara."

"You haven't said much about your family's reaction."

"There isn't much to tell right now. My mom and dad are playing a waiting game. They support me in whatever I do, even if they aren't always crazy about it. That's the way they are."

"What about Brendan and Kelly?"

"Kelly's been out of town, working on a new commission that she and her partner just received, and Brendan's been working on a very tough case."

"Anything that I might have heard of?"

"Probably." Cat paused to sip her coffee. "The Cummings trial."

Mary Alice's eyes widened. "He's involved in *that?*"

"It's his case now."

"How depressing."

"But when he wins," Cat said with sibling pride, "it'll be worth it."

"Is he as confident as you?"

"He has to be or he wouldn't prosecute the case. Nor would the D.A. or the victim trust him as much as they do."

"Speaking of trust—do you trust Rory?"

"With Tara?" Cat took a long, deep sip of her coffee. "Yes."

"What about with you?"

"I doubt that I'll ever really trust him again in that regard. That would be foolish, and I'm no fool." Cat gave her assistant a quizzical smile. "At least I'm not any longer."

"But you don't hate him anymore, do you?"

"Hate Rory?" Cat asked putting down her cup and moving a few feet away from her desk. "Hate him?" She lifted her chin and tilted her head, gazing upward for a moment before she returned her glance to Mary Alice. "I never hated him."

"I thought…"

"That because of what he did I loathed him to that degree?"

"Something like that."

Cat's smile was still there, however faint. "I was hurt, disappointed, and to be truthful, even pissed off later, but hate? I couldn't. Without him I wouldn't have my daughter, and that was worth any personal sacrifice."

"So where do you see this going?"

"I don't know. Depends on a lot of things. As long as I'm not backed into any corners. For right now I'm okay with the way things are."

"And what if he wants more?"

"I'm not part of the package."

"Of course you are," her assistant scoffed. "You're Tara's mother. That automatically makes you a very important part of any package involving your daughter's future."

"I know that, but that's not what I meant," she started to say when the phone rang. Cat answered it. "Hello, The Silver Harp, this is Cat speaking. May I help you?"

"I do believe that you can."

Cat shivered slightly, recognizing that very sexy masculine voice. "In what way?"

Rory leaned back in his office chair, his eyes bright with an inner glow. *By letting me touch you, hold you, make love to you again,* he wanted to say. If he uttered the words, she was sure to slam the phone down on him without hesitation, so he kept his erotic thoughts to himself.

"What are you doing on Saturday?"

"I'm not sure," she said. "Why?"

"Then check your calendar, and I'll call you back."

"What did you have in mind?"

"I thought Tara might fancy the odd bit of riding."

Cat couldn't keep the bittersweet smile from widening on her lips. Every so often, Rory came out with an expression that was so purely the other side of the Atlantic.

"One of the staff here was telling me about a riding stable not far from where you live. Maybe a half hour or so away. Gentle mounts for children. And," he laughed, "adults."

She hadn't been on a horse in years. Since she was a teenager, if she recalled correctly. And she'd been meaning to take Tara for lessons. One of the advantages of living in Chester County, southeastern Pennsylvania's premier horse country.

"I thought you might enjoy it too."

It was so tempting.

"Come on. You know you want to."

His voice was so incredibly seductive. "What makes you think I can't handle a faster, harder ride?"

Rory stifled the groan that almost escaped his lips. He knew what she meant by her remark; trouble was, her words conjured up a different image to him, more explicit, much more sensual. "I'll take your word that you can.'' He glanced at the photo he'd taken from Cat's desk, which now rested on his.

"We could make a day of it. I've been told that the inn they have there has wonderful food.''

"Wait a minute. Is this Colby Farm?''

"Yes. How'd you know?''

"There was an article about the inn and stables several months ago in the *Inquirer*'s travel section. It sounded like a fabulous place to visit.''

"Then let's do it.''

"Let me talk to Tara about it.''

"Then I'll call you later tonight.''

"Make it tomorrow morning.''

"May I ask why?''

Cat mentally debated telling him that it really wasn't any of his business where she was going or what she was going to do with her time; but what good would that accomplish? None whatsoever. "I'm doing dinner at my parents, then we're going to the local Harvest Festival, so it'll be late when I get home.''

Relief flooded through him. For a moment he thought she might have had a date with another man. "What's this festival all about?''

"It's an annual thing,'' she explained. "Streets are closed off in town, food and craft vendors are set up, there's usually a band, and activities for the kids. It's used as a fund-raiser for several local community groups.''

"I don't think I've heard about it.''

"It's fairly new,'' she said, "only about five years or so old. Tara really loves it, and so it's become an annual event for us.''

Rory considered this information, his mind already

formulating a plan of action. "Then I will call you tomorrow," he promised. "Have a good time tonight."

"I intend to," she said as she hung up the phone. She had almost invited him, a move that might have been misconstrued on his part. Too much too soon, her heart warned. She wanted to be careful not to slide into dangerous territory. Lapse into something that had nowhere to go. She shouldn't even consider the ride either, but it was something she wanted, both for herself and Tara. Besides, she doubted Rory would fit in at a street fair. It just wasn't his style at all.

Rory contemplated the view from his window. Trees were starting to deepen to ripe fall colors, patches of red, gold, burgundy and orange. The air was crisper; the temperature cooler. Time was not standing still, waiting for his command. It moved inexorably forward, pushing past human hesitations and concerns. Always, always forward.

He had to do the same. To stand idly by was to risk failure, risk disappointment. And that, to him, wasn't an option.

"Are you having a good time, honey?"

"Uh-huh," Tara answered with a bright smile as she bit into the crusty shell of the caramel apple on a stick. She was watching a street clown perform, laughing at his antics.

The town of Cedar Hill was alive with the spirit of the festival. Traffic was blocked off of the main road so that pedestrians could stroll along the street, visit the vendors that were set up along the sidewalk, or along the cobbled thoroughfare. There were booths selling fresh and dried floral displays, some with handmade crafts such as wreaths and items for the home, others with food and drink. Cat held tightly to Tara's hand, sipping a paper mug of hot spiced tea with the other as they made their way through the crowd.

She was admiring the needlework of one woman who had a table full of embroidered goods when she heard a voice behind her.

"Fancy that, do you?"

Cat's head swiveled to the right, and she saw Rory standing there, a disarming smile on his lips.

"Rory, hi!" said Tara enthusiastically, letting go of her mother's hand to greet the man warmly.

He bent down and scooped the child into his arms. "And what are you eating, my lady fair?"

Tara giggled at the pet name Rory had lately taken to calling her. "A caramel apple. Want a bite?"

"I'd love one."

Cat felt a small twinge of jealousy spark within herself at the easy way Tara shared her food with the until-several-weeks-ago-stranger, who'd also insisted that the little girl call him by his first name.

She watched as Rory took a hearty bite, his white teeth clamping onto the hard caramel shell, easily removing a piece.

"Delicious," he pronounced, much to the little girl's delight.

"What are you doing here?" Cat demanded softly, her face showing her surprise at his appearance.

"Enjoying myself," he replied.

"You know what I mean."

"Come to see for myself just what this fair is."

"You've never been to one?" Tara asked, enjoying her vantage point high atop in his arms, waving to a school friend.

"No," Rory admitted, shifting his attention to Tara. "Have I missed much?"

"Oh yes," she stated earnestly. "Lots and lots of things."

"Like what?"

"Caramel apples, for one."

Rory chuckled at her quickness. "And what else?"

"All the neat stuff you can see here," she said importantly. "There's a woman who comes every year. She makes cloth dolls that are dressed in costume. I got one last time that was dressed in colonial clothes. This year Mommy said that I can get the Mr. Doll so that Polly won't be lonely."

"I take it Polly is your doll's name?"

"Yes. Polly Kildare. She shares my last name."

He flicked a glance at Cat. "Does she now? And what would you name your Mr. doll?"

"Percy."

Rory lifted one black eyebrow. "Where does that come from?"

"Mommy read me the story of the *Scarlet Pimpernel,*" she said. "His name was Percy, and he was a hero who got to do cool things like wear disguises and fight with a sword."

"Will Percy have a last name?"

Tara looked her father square in the face, her voice suddenly shy. "Can I borrow yours?"

Rory heard Cat's quick intake of breath. "Of course you can, my lady fair."

"Goodie." She gave Rory a quick hug. "Mommy told me that you are gonna take us riding on Saturday. I can't wait."

While Tara attacked her apple treat again, Rory addressed Cat. "You never answered my question. Do you fancy some of this lady's work?"

"And what if I did?"

He resisted the impulse to say that he would cheerfully buy it for her. "No reason, just asking."

Relieved, she responded, "I thought it would make a great gift for my sister, Kelly. She loves things like these."

"Then you should get whatever you want for her," he advised. "If not, you'll regret it, and there's nothing as sad as regret."

She looked at him, trying to read the expression in his dark blue eyes, but Rory focused his attention on Tara, pointing out a nearby food stand. Turning her head, Cat purchased the items she wanted, adding something for herself as well.

"Mommy?"

Cat turned and was struck anew at the resemblance between man and child. What gave her a significant twinge was that they looked so right together. "Yes, Tara?"

"Can we go listen to the music?"

"Sure." She held out her arms, claiming her child from Rory.

He released Tara, putting her back down on the ground.

"Come with us," the child pleaded.

Cat took Tara's hand again. "We can't monopolize Mr. Sullivan's time tonight, darling. He may have other plans."

"None that can't be altered for a pair of fair ladies," he answered.

"Then come on," Tara begged. "My nan and pop are there too."

Rory fixed his glance on Cat. "Your parents?"

"Does that change your mind?"

"No." It could prove awkward, he acknowledged, but he wasn't going to let the prospect stop him. After all, they might one day be his in-laws, so he'd better get used to being in their company.

They strolled the cobbled street, looking like the perfect family, until they found the area where the band was set up. Chairs were set up, and a spot cleared for dancing. Several couples were already on the floor, moving to the up-tempo beat, a variation of a currently popular swing number.

Cat stood, Tara in front of her, aware of how close Rory was to her. The press of people forced him to move closer to her, their arms touching. She couldn't pull away without looking like a fool, as if his touch bothered her. Because it did.

Rory glanced at his reluctant companion, letting his eyes look their fill. She was staring straight ahead. He liked the twin set she wore, the fine material of the caramel-brown sweater clinging to her shapely curves. Eyes dipping lower, he admired the way the short cream-colored wool skirt she wore showed off her fabulous legs, the same legs he vividly remembered clinging to him, teasing him, taking him.

"Cat, over here," called a deep masculine voice when there was a break in the music.

The three of them turned in unison, searching out the speaker. It was Cat's father, seated next to an older version of Cat, some feet away.

Tara grabbed Rory's hand. "Now you can meet my nan and pop."

"I've already had that privilege, my lady fair."

"Okay," the child answered, dashing for the sanctuary of her grandparents.

Rory watched as the older man swept the little girl into his arms, nuzzling her neck, making the child giggle with delight. The woman took her turn next, pulling Tara into her lap, hugging her close. "They seem to adore her," he commented to Cat.

"Does that surprise you?" she asked.

"No, not really. It's just that not having known either of my sets of grandparents, I'm happy to see that she hasn't missed that."

Cat couldn't help but be touched by that revelation and by the thread of envy she heard in his voice. Damn it, just when she was fixed on keeping her emotional distance from the man, he went and said something that pulled her in, tapped her wellspring of compassion. This was way too dangerous.

"I think they're waiting."

Cat glanced in her parents' direction, both of whom were watching her with questioning faces.

"Reluctant as I normally am to quote an Englishman, even a genius, I find that I must. 'Once more into the breech, dear friend.'"

Cat couldn't help it, laughter bubbled up inside her and escaped.

Rory grinned. He'd missed that laugh in the intervening years they'd been apart. Missed the sound, the texture, the way the color of her eyes deepened.

"Mom, Dad, you remember Rory Sullivan, don't you?" Cat held her breath after asking the rhetorical question.

Her mother was politeness itself as she extended her hand. "We meet again."

"Hello." Rory took her hand, slipping his other over

top of their linked hands. "The years have been kind to you, ma'am. You look rather more like Cat's older sister instead of her mother."

Mary Kildare smiled. "Been kissing that Blarney stone, have you, Mr. Sullivan?"

"I doubt that a cold piece of stone's been occupying his life exclusively these past years, Mary," her husband said in a chilly tone. "My guess is that many an Irish lass has wept herself silly in his wake."

"Not so many as you'd think," Rory said as he responded to the barb.

"Don't be modest, lad."

"Trust me I'm not being modest." Rory held out his hand, not sure that her father would take it.

"Trust *you?*" Brian Kildare said with a false smile, gripping the younger man's hand and squeezing hard. "Not likely."

Cat stepped in before all-out war, or at least a nasty skirmish could ensue.

"Daddy, please."

"Relax, sweetheart," he said, favoring her with a smile as he released Rory's hand. "I won't read him his rights."

"Thanks."

"Is my pop arresting Rory?" Tara asked, overhearing what her grandfather said.

"Of course not, sweetheart," Cat assured her. "He was just making a joke, that's all."

Tara seemed satisfied with her mother's explanation.

"But, that doesn't mean…" Brian continued.

Cat interrupted him. "Later, okay?"

Her father acquiesced. "Whatever you want, sweetheart."

Rory observed the continued closeness between Cat

and her folks; he even understood their reluctance to
welcome him with open arms. To them he was the vile
seducer of their precious daughter, the man who left her
to raise a child alone. That he hadn't known probably
didn't mean much to them, especially considering he
couldn't be sure even now what he would have done.

But he knew now what he wanted to do.

He approached Cat. "Dance with me."

"What?"

"Dance with me," he repeated, holding out his hand.

It would be foolish to say yes, she thought, but she
did it anyway.

They moved through the gathered crowd, the lights
that were strung around the trees on either side of the
street gleaming softly, giving off an almost enchanted
glow.

A sultry female lead singer was holding the crowd
captive with her dark, smoky-voiced rendition of "All
The Way."

Rory took Cat in his arms, and they moved to the
music. At first she was stiff, holding herself back. Then,
seconds later, she relaxed, giving in to the rhythm of the
music, swaying back and forth.

Of all the men that she'd ever danced with, she realized at that moment, it was with Rory that she felt the
most comfortable, the most free, the most female.

He held her close, arms wrapped securely around her
form. That same form that was pressed against his, in-
timately. Rory wondered if she could feel the hard evidence of his desire for her? A desire that rose with each
breath, each movement.

The song ended, and when Cat made to step away
from his arms, he tightened his hold. "Not yet," he mur-

mured in a silky tone. He couldn't let go, not after all these years, not after all his dreams.

The singer began another ballad, her vocal skill commanding as she poured her talents into a smashing rendition of the pop classic "The Look of Love."

The lyrics wove through Cat's head, saturating her brain. The simple power of the song invaded her skin, sharpening her senses. So sharp were they that she felt a warning bell go off in her head.

"You'll have to excuse me," she managed to say. "I'm feeling very tired right now."

"Tired?" God, not now, he prayed, not when he wanted to hold her for hours to come.

"Yes, it's been a long day."

"Is that all?"

"What else could there be?" she asked as he released her. Cat backed away, needing to put distance between them. Being so close was to be filled with sensory memories, the kind that insidiously burrowed into the empty spaces of her heart and grew like an emotional cancer.

Rory walked her back to where her parents sat with Tara, the little girl finding it hard to keep her eyes open.

"We've got to get home," Cat said, bending down to scoop up her daughter from her mother's protective arms.

"Do you want me to carry her?" Rory asked. "She looks too heavy for you."

"Not necessary," Cat said. "I'm used to taking care of her."

"What about a ride home then?"

"We'll see to that," Brian Kildare chimed in, getting up from his chair and moving, along with his wife, to stand next to Cat.

Rory didn't need a telegraph to receive the message that they were sending.

Tara muttered a sleepy "Goodbye" in Rory's general direction.

"Sweet dreams, my lady fair." He saw her small mouth curve into a smile as she drifted back off to sleep. To Cat he said, "I'll call you tomorrow and finalize the plans for Saturday." He then watched them depart, the ache in his arms and in his heart intensifying with every step that Cat took away from him.

"Hi. Care to dance?"

Rory turned his head at the feminine invitation. "Thanks, but no thanks. I'm just leaving."

"The fair's open for a few more hours. What's your hurry?" the girl asked with a pretty pout.

"Doesn't matter," he said.

She was persistent. "We could have a really good time," she insisted, stepping closer and laying a hand on his arm.

There was a time in his life when he would have welcomed the appeal of a young woman like her, one eager and oh-so-willing to spread her sexual wings. He could have accepted her open-handed flirtation, whiled away a few pleasant hours in her company and both of them would have parted happy and satisfied.

And that would have happened BC.

Before Cat.

Still, there was nothing stopping him from accepting what was so readily offered.

Nothing but his heart.

"Well, ain't he got nerve?" Brian Kildare commented as he drove the short distance from the festival to the Kildare home.

"You'll wake Tara, Daddy," Cat said softly from the back seat.

"I won't," he promised, "but I won't keep silent either."

"Why change now?" Mary asked, giving her husband a lovingly ironic glance.

"I kept my mouth shut—" he threw his wife a quick glance "—well, almost shut, the last time. I thought then that he was much too sophisticated for our girl, and only out for himself, which he was. Now he's back, oozing charm just like before. What's he want?"

Her father sounded just like Brendan, Cat thought. Suspicious. Distrustful. Cautious.

Everything she should be.

And she was.

Just not as vehemently as the males in her family.

Except that little by little, Roy was breaking down, a solitary brick at a time, her outer defense wall. Not a lot, but cracks were definitely occurring.

Her mind floated back to the music. How she loved dancing with him again. A guilty pleasure she savored and relived all the way home.

She was too keyed up to sleep.

Checking on Tara, who was sound asleep, Cat padded back to her bedroom. The night had turned colder, the temperature dropping rapidly, so she shut her open windows and scrambled back to her comfortable, oversized bed, burrowing under the comforter.

Reaching for the novel she was reading, Cat settled in with what she hoped would take her mind from the source of her sleeplessness. It was a new historical romance from local author Kate Reeves. Set in Ireland, it was a sweeping tale of love lost and reclaimed, called *Return to Forever*.

Cat smiled as she glanced once again at the dedication page. Hers was one of the names listed there. Reeves had come to her shop about two years ago looking for research books, and one of the ones that Cat had recommended had been Rory's. The two women had hit it off, and when the author received her advance copies, she'd sent an autographed one to Cat.

It wasn't hard to figure out who the author had in mind when she created her hero. The description of the wild, reckless, passionate and handsome Irish rebel leader was a dead ringer for Rory.

Cat never considered *not* reading the book. After the first page, she was hooked and there was no turning back.

Later, she fell sleep, dreaming of him in this new persona, a delightful smile on her lips.

Chapter Seven

"I want you to marry me."

If Cat could have seen the look on her own face, she would have witnessed a visual definition of the word *stunned*.

"*Marry?*" If he had asked her seven years ago, her answer would have been yes, instantly, without hesitation, without fear.

But now?

"Why?"

Rory knew he'd caught her by surprise. Hell, he'd caught himself by surprise. Yet there it was. The words poured out as if released from a long period of confinement. They were sharing coffee in her den, relaxing after a long day spent together with their daughter. The visit to the Colby Farm was a success. Tara had loved riding the pony, taking to it as if she'd done it all her life. She had wheedled a promise from both of them to bring her back the following week. She was a charmer, he thought, winding both of them around her finger with ease.

His daughter indeed.

"You don't have to give me an answer right away," he said calmly. "Take a few days to think about it."

Cat was still in shock. "You haven't answered my question, Rory. Why?"

He sounded sincere. "For Tara's sake." And for my own, he added silently.

"And how would that benefit Tara?" Cat asked, glad that her daughter was getting ready for bed and out of earshot of this conversation.

"By having her family together."

Cat argued, "She already has a family."

"I don't mean *yours*," Rory stressed, "but *ours*."

"There is no *ours*," she retorted.

"There could be, if you'd say yes."

"Could. That's a long way from should."

"Not that long if you want it badly enough," he pointed out.

"What I want is my daughter's happiness," Cat stressed, "first and foremost."

His voice was low. "And you think that I don't?"

"I don't have a clue, Rory." Cat got up from her seat on the sofa, closed the pocket door and turned to face him. "You come back into my life almost as if you'd never left, pretending that it's been barely months instead of years."

"That's not true."

"True or not, it's how it seems. And now you want to be a part of Tara's life? For how long? Until a better offer comes along?"

That stung. "For the rest of her life, if you'll have me."

Her green eyes were skeptical. "You can, if you're truly serious, be a part of Tara's life, right now," she offered. "Without having to marry me to do it."

"But it wouldn't be the same." You wouldn't be my wife, he wanted to say.

"Why wouldn't it?"

Rory paused, trying to formulate another reason, one that he could utter. "You've done a great job, Cat, but together we can do an even better one."

She gave him an arch look. "How?"

"By being her mother and father. All the time. Not just on special outings."

Where, she wondered, had this proposal for domestic bliss come from? It wasn't like the man she knew. "This is kind of sudden, isn't it?"

"I've been thinking along this line for the last several weeks now. Falling deeper with each passing day, under our daughter's spell." And that was true, he realized. "I understand just what she means to me. How she's added to my life, not subtracted."

Cat took a deep breath, then slowly exhaled. "I wish that I could believe you."

Rory stood up, approached her. "You can."

Yet her heart was telling her she couldn't. He'd let her down once before and more than likely he would again if she let him. He seemed sincere, but how could she really tell? "I only have your word for that."

"Which isn't good enough, is it?"

Bluntly, she answered. "Exactly."

"Then would you agree to a trial marriage?"

"Trial?"

"To adjust."

"We could have a trial engagement," she countered.

"Not acceptable," he said. "It's all or nothing, Cat.

You and I can't live together, try and build something if it's too easy to walk away.''

"That's your department," she responded.

"Touché.''

Her verbal dart had hit home, though it didn't make her feel any better slinging it. What surprised her was that he didn't bother to deny it.

He moved closer, to within inches of her face, her body, ignoring her sharp words, trying a different tactic. "She wouldn't be forced to choose if we were together. Tara would have two people who cared for her, living under the same roof. A mother and a father, albeit,'' he said in a slightly mocking tone, "one who is late to the game.

"But late doesn't mean disinterested. I've got a lot of catching up to do. Granted. With your help, we can make it a smooth transition.''

"You make it sound like a business merger.''

"That's the farthest thing from my mind.'' He reached out his hand and touched her cheek, feathering his index finger along her skin. "I want this to be a *real* marriage.''

"And how do you define that?'' She couldn't take her eyes from his, trapped by the intensity she saw there.

"Us,'' he whispered. "Together in the truest sense of man and wife.''

The look on his face was easy for Cat to read. He meant they would have a sexual relationship. Again. Husband and wife. Sleep together. Lie in his arms and let him love her. Let him become an intimate part of her life again.

"You'd want to sleep with me?''

"Of course. Just like any other married couple who make love.''

Make love. She'd made love to him in another life-time. Given her heart and soul. He, however, had had sex. Love, to her, wasn't something you walked away from. With sex you just picked up and went, no strings. Because it didn't matter. One body was just as com-forting as another. Hadn't he proved it to her? He talked about staying, about building a family—but could he? Would he? Did he really mean it?

A rumble of thunder echoed across the sky, shaking the window.

A warning? An omen?

Cat forced her eyes to look away, to focus on some-thing else. She watched as the rain broke; a steady down-pour let loose with a stinging intensity.

Instantly, it brought to her mind memories of another day—another downpour....

They were soaked, both having been caught in a sud-den, late-afternoon storm. She'd visited him on campus, and they were having lunch at a nearby restaurant, the day warm and muggy. When they came out, it was pour-ing.

Laughing, they made a dash back to his office. Once inside, Rory shut the door and turned the key, locking it securely, the broadest of smiles on his mouth.

"We've got to get you out of those wet clothes."

"I can't," she said. "Besides, I don't have anything else to wear."

Rory opened the door to his office closet. Inside, along with an extra tweed jacket and a fresh shirt, was a sweater, a thick, navy blue cardigan. "Here." He re-moved the sweater and held it out to her. "Put this on."

"That's okay," she said, rubbing her arms to remove the moisture, which was made cooler by the air-conditioning. "I'll be fine."

"You'll get a chill."

"No I won't."

"Do it for me," he coaxed.

"All right," she said, unable to refuse him when he used that tone of voice or looked at her that way.

Cat turned her back, and Rory almost chuckled. He found her sense of modesty sweetly attractive. In an era where nothing was held back, she retained her own code of propriety.

He watched as she peeled off her clinging white T-shirt dress, pulling it over her head so that he saw, before she put on the sweater, a glimpse of the back of her. A small birthmark. A few gold-dusted freckles. White cotton bra and panties. Nothing exotic. Nothing fancy. But on her, they were as sexy as hell to him.

Cat pirouetted around, clad in his sweater; it hung on her, large and enveloping. She'd pushed back the overly long sleeves. It came to midthigh on her, affording him a great view of her shapely legs. He noticed that she still wore her high-heeled white sandals.

A phrase he'd heard someone say before popped into his mind: He could eat her up with a spoon.

Or, even better, with his mouth.

With a sweeping fling of his hand, Rory sent all the material on his desk flying, scattering the contents—papers, books, pens—to the floor.

Her eyes widened knowingly. "You can't be serious."

"Oh, but I am," he said, stripping off his sodden shirt and khaki paints. "Very."

With that, Rory pulled Cat into his arms, unbuttoning the sweater, gently peeling it back. "God, you're beautiful," he whispered, his voice raw with need.

He lifted her onto the desk, bending down to remove

her sandals. Carefully, he slipped the shoe off one foot, holding her steady, then lightly massaging the arch.

Cat leaned back, relaxing, enjoying the feel of his hands on her skin. Then they slid up her leg, learning the texture of her calf, the curve of her thigh.

"Rory," she sighed, her breath coming faster, ignoring the hardness of the oak beneath her.

"What do you want?" he asked, his mouth on her stomach, working upward.

"You know."

His voice was low, husky, seducing. "Tell me."

"You." She wet her lips. "Now." She grasped his arms. "Here."

Hot. Fast. Hard. Their lovemaking was an explosion of passion that utterly drained her, leaving her limp. It was like the storm, wild and powerful.

"Cat?"

She snapped back to the present, her cheeks warm. Why couldn't she stop these memories? Or better still, ignore them?

"Yes."

"Will you think about it?"

Why wasn't she telling him that it was impossible? That she couldn't marry someone she didn't love. Because she didn't love him, she told herself. Hadn't for years. Want him? Well, that was another story. Want wasn't as easy to let go. It was an itch that craved scratching. A hunger that demanded its meal of choice.

"Give me a few days."

"I said that I would." The smile on his mouth told her without words that he too was remembering a particular rainy-day afternoon delight.

Damn! Was she that transparent?

"We could make it work."

"You're so sure?"

"Because I know the woman you are."

"Not anymore you don't."

"Yes, I do. If you promise something, then you'll do it, to the best of your ability. If you give yourself over to something, then you do it full throttle."

"I like to think so."

"Believe it."

"But what about love?"

"What about it?" he countered. "Love will follow later. We have a lot to build on. Our history. Our child. Similar tastes, likes and dislikes. An understanding of what we both get out of this—a family for our daughter. People have married for less. And divorced with much more. Compromise is a small price to pay to give her a complete family, don't you think?" He waited for her response, not revealing his inner truth, that he was already in love with her. That if she would only let him, he'd show her how much. Allow him to make up for lost time. Erase the sorrow.

But he couldn't confide that right now. Cat wouldn't believe he was telling her the truth. Hell, why should she? He'd said he loved her before, and then he let her slip through his fingers. Trust had been lost. Rory was smart enough to realize you didn't get that back overnight. It would come slowly. Daily. Inch by inch. Then one day, when she was ready, it would be there. Waiting. She'd know it and so would he.

She needed some space. "I'd like you to leave now."

"If that's what you really want."

Her green eyes were shadowed, wary. Where once they were open to him, now they were locked; and he no longer had the key. No, he thought, amending the observation. He might still have a key, but the lock had been changed.

Cat replied, "Yes, it is."

He was about to go when he gave in to a whim. Quickly, before she could protest, he captured her chin in one hand and then held her still for his swift kiss.

"There," he said. "Think about that, too."

Cat stood there, regaining her equilibrium, her mind reeling from the kiss. Though it had been quick, it was like a sharp, jagged flash of lightning, illuminating the sky with its momentary brilliance.

She raised her hand and lightly touched her lips with her fingertips. Whatever else, they did still have that.

She heard her name called. A voice summoning her from the realm of sleep with a seductiveness, a possessiveness so strong that she couldn't ignore it.

Her room was covered in fog, a cool, clinging dampness that enveloped her. Rising from her bed, she ran blindly through the swirls of mist, searching for the source of that persuasive tone, knowing that she had to find it. Like a phantom, it seemed always beyond her grasp, for as soon as she thought that she was close, it changed direction, so that she had to run again to find it.

Cat stopped to catch her breath, her sides aching from the futile search, when she heard it. Her name was repeated again, with the additional words, "Trust me." It echoed in her brain like a litany.

Where was he?

From the depths of the mist a figure approached her, cutting through the fog with ease.

"You!" she exclaimed.

His smile was confident and supremely masculine. "Whom did you expect?"

She started to run, this time away from the voice, from the dawning comprehension of what he meant, but her feet were tangled in the swirls of vapor that rose up around her. "Stay away!"

"I tried," he responded.

"I don't want you."

He laughed. "That's a lie and you know it."

She could feel the heat in her cheeks as she acceded to the truth in what he said.

"You can't deny it, Cat, much as you might wish to. Be honest with yourself, with me. Acknowledge the feelings, *your* feelings. Give in."

He moved so that he was within inches of her body. She saw the fire of unbanked passion in his eyes. He was waiting for her, silently issuing the invitation.

No use to pretend. There was only the two of them. No one else would know.

Cat accepted.

Her hand reached forward, then halted. She blinked in astonishment. He stood before her wearing clothes conjured from her imagination. She recognized the garments because only a few days prior, she had been flipping through the pages of a specialty catalog, and she had imagined him in these very same clothes.

"I wore them for you," he explained, as if reading her mind.

For her. With that thought Cat smiled her pleasure. He did look handsome. More than any man had a right to be. Her fingertips traced the deep, dark blue velvet collar of the smoking jacket; felt the rich texture of the material in autumn hues; tightened on the velvet belt that held it together. Keeping her eyes locked with his, she began to unknot the belt, pulling it loose, exposing the warm skin of his torso underneath. She slid her fingers along his rib cage, across the fine hairs that angled his chest. Her fingertips felt the electric current between his flesh and hers, alive and vibrant, pulsing with a power all its own.

Tension was building in her body. The coils of desire were lifting her, pressing her to explore, to accept, to surrender.

He shrugged out of the jacket, letting it be swallowed up by the mist. "Don't stop," he commanded softly.

Cat couldn't even if she wanted to. This was an inevitable reaction.

Her mouth pressed against his, savoring the warmth she found there. Her tongue traced the contours of his lips before her own were persuaded to join with him in their mating ritual.

How could she have ever imagined that she could live the rest of her life without this? It would be like living without sunlight, without air.

"Please," she moaned as his mouth feasted on the slender column of her throat.

"Please what?" he asked, continuing his sensual assault on her neck, nibbling, tasting.

"Take me...now."

Her plea forced him to stop. He cupped her jaw in his large hands, his fingers rubbing rhythmically across her skin. "I am."

"I need..." She paused.

"What?" he said.

"To feel you..."

"Where?"

"Inside me."

"I've never left," he said with a smile.

"Prove it," she begged.

"Gladly," he responded, taking her hand, placing it on the drawstring that held together the pajama bottoms of indigo blue silk he wore. "Release me."

She did, marveling at the supreme grace and power of his virile body.

"Your turn," he said, proceeding to take his time with the tiny buttons of her brushed-cotton gown, until all were free from their respective buttonholes. The material hugged her breasts, revealing only the slopes, the rest still hidden from view.

It was her hand that pulled the cotton apart, that pushed it down her arms and off her hips to fall, pooling, at her feet.

His dark gaze dropped; she could feel the tightening of her nipples in response; longed for the sensual touch of his long-fingered hand on her flesh, sliding and cupping, fondling and caressing.

Cat lowered her lids for an instant. When she raised them again, he was gone...vanished...swallowed up by the mist.

And she was left empty. Once again, alone.

Cat called out to him as she began to run through the ever-increasing fog. "Rory. *Rory!*"

Cat's eyes flew open. Her heart was racing. She was in her own bedroom, and judging by the light filtering in the window, it was almost time to get up.

It had all been a dream.

A frustrating, exacerbating excursion into an illusory world.

Cat threw back the comforter and slipped her arms into her comfy chenille robe. It had seemed so real, so achingly real. She had been ready to give herself to him without hesitation, without thought for the consequences of her actions, just like before.

In her dream state, she'd put aside her constant doubts, suspended her fears, and followed her instincts, nearly capitulated to the desires she thought she had suppressed so well.

She would have to be on her guard, careful not to allow herself to be swayed by fanciful imaginings, dangerous reminiscences. She was drawn to him, drawn to the magnetic radius of his special, unique male aura. The temptation to give herself to his embrace was strong. When she felt the intense pressure of his hard mouth on the softness of hers, she knew she'd wanted to allow him entrance. Wanted to feel the enchantment again, the sweet magic he practiced. A part of her mind wanted to reach out and grab a handful of heaven, even if it was only hers for a few minutes.

But heaven, like everything else, had its price, and she'd already paid for her share once before.

Her glance fell to the high, cut-glass vase filled with roses that sat on the top of her long chest of drawers. Every few days, since Rory's return, a fresh delivery came to the store and to her home, with another smaller selection of flowers for Tara, who got such a kick out of the treat.

She could almost believe that he was wooing her, as he had so long ago. But that would be a mistake.

She ventured over and inhaled the fragrance, then picked up one of the long-stemmed beauties from its container, pricking her finger in the process on a sharp barb that should have been removed.

Touching her tongue to the droplet of blood that formed at the tip of her index finger, Cat licked it clean, then snapped the offending barb off so that the incident wouldn't be repeated.

Cat's mouth formed a bittersweet curve. Memories possessed thorns too. Ones that weren't so easily removed.

"So, why the emergency call?" asked Kelly Kildare as her sister joined her for lunch at her office in a reconverted warehouse just outside of town.

Cat made room on the old trestle table, clearing off the stacks of rolled blueprints that littered the top. She also removed the stack of books and computer printouts that added to the clutter, pushing them down to the other end. When she was done, she opened the large brown paper tote bag she carried and proceeded to lay out an assortment of food for lunch.

Kelly, her office bathed by sunlight, which streamed in through the many windows and skylights, joined her sister.

"I just needed to talk to someone today to sort things out, and you were who I thought of."

"It's about Rory, isn't it?"

"Mom told you, right?"

Kelly shook her head, the shoulder-length pageboy cut swinging around her neck. "Brendan."

"My next guess," Cat said as she removed her outer sweater, hanging it on the brass tree in the corner before taking a seat.

Kelly helped her older-sister-by-two-years open the foil-wrapped sandwiches and picked out the one she wanted, along with a large bottle of water. "He was concerned about you."

Cat took a healthy bite of her Italian hoagie. "What'd he say?"

"That the man who'd once tried to ruin your life had come back to town."

Cat wiped her mouth with a paper napkin. "Objection. Prejudicial to the facts of the case."

At the pointed reference to their older brother's profession, both women laughed.

"Seriously," Kelly said, adding a bit of salt to her turkey, ham and cheese sandwich. "He was worried."

"He needn't be."

'But that's Brendan." Kelly cast a glance at the fax machine on her desk, listening to it spit out pages.

"Something important?" Cat asked as her sister's dark head turned back in her direction.

"Just some ideas that I'm waiting for regarding another project that I'm thinking about taking after I finish this one."

"Something special?"

Kelly laughed, a sparkling sound, much like Cat's. "Could be. I've been offered a chance to design not only an office-building complex, but a home as well in an historic district."

Cat's interest was perked. "Where?"

"Australia."

Cat's eyes widened, realizing what a coup this would be for her sister's fledgling business if she won the commission. It would be her first truly international project, something, if it happened, that would garner Kelly's company even more prestige and more commissions. "How did this come about?"

"Through Aunt Pat actually. When Mom and Dad were visiting her in Melbourne, one of her stepsons happened to stop by for a visit, too. It seems that he mentioned he was going to develop property that he'd bought years ago and was looking for just the right firm of architects to bring his ideas into being.''

''Which of her stepsons?'' Her aunt had married a widower with four sons.

''The second-oldest, Rick.''

''So you were nominated? Congratulations.''

''I don't have the deal yet,'' Kelly said, wolfing down a crunchy dill pickle with a few quick bites.

''When he sees your work, I'm sure he'll want you to do it.''

''Well, I faxed him a few sketches and shipped him a set of completed project pictures, to give him an idea of the work we do here.''

''So you'd have to go there?''

''That's the plan if he likes my stuff. I'm hoping that he'll get back to me soon. You know how I am about lining up work. I like to know what I'm doing next once I've completed the current project.'' Kelly paused, giving her sister a pointed look. ''But that's not why you called me, is it?''

Cat shook her head in denial. ''Not that I'm not interested,'' she stated.

Kelly reached out her hand and gave her sister's a reassuring squeeze. ''I know. So tell me.''

''Rory asked me to marry him last night.''

Kelly was about to take another bite of her sandwich and changed her mind. ''Marry?''

''Uh-huh,'' Cat answered. ''Can you believe that?''

''Why?''

''He said that he wants to give Tara a real family.''

''And you don't think so?''

''Why would he want to be married to someone who doesn't love him, even for the sake of a child, when he doesn't have to?''

Kelly asked her delicately, "You don't still love him, do you, Cat?"

Cat responded with, "Do you still love Keith?"

Kelly pursed her lips. "That's a different story."

"Could you ever forgive him?"

"No." It was a stark, final answer.

"You're sure?"

"Very."

"Well, maybe you can see my dilemma. Rory wants us to be one big happy family. A *real* family."

"And what do you want?"

"For my daughter to be happy."

"What about your happiness?" Kelly asked. "Would marrying your daughter's father make *you* happy?"

"Years ago, yes. Now…"

"Tara won't be happy if you're miserable." Kelly paused, taking a sip from the still-chilled bottle of water. "Have you told her yet about Rory being her father?"

"No. I have wanted to, but there never seemed to be a right time."

"You're gonna have to soon."

"I know. Last night, as she was getting ready for bed, saying her prayers, I heard her add Rory's name to her list."

Kelly quickly read her sister's face. "That got to you, didn't it?"

"Yes," Cat answered. "More than I thought it could."

"But? I hear a but in there somewhere."

"Suppose I don't agree, and he threatens to try and get custody from me?"

"What judge would give it to him? You're her mother and you've been her caregiver since she was born."

"Kelly, he's rich. Get real. Money has been known to buy a little thing like a custody case before."

"Less likely when your brother's an assistant D.A. though. Has Rory hinted that he'd do that?"

"No."

"Then don't worry about it for right now. Concentrate on what you want."

"Suppose I don't have a clue? All I can think of is doing what's best for Tara. Maybe having a mother and father together would be best for her."

Kelly focused her razor-sharp blue eyes on her sister. "How about doing what's best for Cat? The rest will follow."

Chapter Eight

He wanted an answer.

She should have just said no and been done with it. That she was considering his proposal at all indicated she had taken leave of her senses. Completely lost her mind. Or at best, seriously misplaced it.

How could she think even remotely about saying yes? After all the hurt. All the years.

Because of her daughter. Each passing day brought Tara closer to her father. Now that Cat had allowed that, could she make him keep his distance, keep up the pretense that he was only an old family friend, that he wasn't Tara's father?

She grappled daily with those questions and more.

If she married him, there were no guarantees that it would be happily-ever-after. Hell, she couldn't imagine it being that way in any event, not with all the history between them.

Cat sat propped up against the thick pillows on her bed, relaxing with her second cup of morning coffee. Tara had spent the night with Cat's cousin Maureen and her family and was due back later this morning. Maureen's eldest daughter, a year older than Tara, had celebrated her birthday last night and Maureen had held a big party, insisting that Tara stay over and visit longer with her cousins.

Seeing the pleasure on Tara's face at the mention of a sleep-over, Cat had readily agreed. As much as she loved her daughter, she also enjoyed the occasional free hour to herself. She took a long, hot bath when she came home, soaking away her cares, if even for a short time. Ate when she pleased. Went to bed early and spent half the night reading Kate Reeves's latest book. Lost herself in Ireland of old, caught up in the romantic spell that the talented author wove.

And thought of Rory.

Especially when she read certain passages of the romance. Visualized herself and him as the hero and heroine made love. Cat had closed her eyes and experienced again the passion and the sharing, the anguish and the joy when the heroine boldly demanded that the hero touch her.

"I want your hands on my body. That's all I've dreamt about since the first day we met. It's all that I've thought about. How they would feel. How I would feel. Don't make me wait any longer. Do it. Now."

Cat admitted to herself that she missed that. The knowing touch. The abandon of giving yourself to a lover skilled in pleasure. The intense hunger, satisfied only by the ultimate surrender.

She was still young. Thirty-two her last birthday. There was plenty of time for her to meet someone else.

Fall in love again. Have a happy marriage. Or a reasonably good relationship.

Could she set aside the possibilities of her could-be life for what may or may not be best for her child? Would it do her daughter more harm than good to see her mother in a marriage devoid of real lasting love?

Or would the fact that her mother and father were together compensate?

Cat was still considering that moments later when she heard a car pull up in the driveway. Certain that it was Maureen bringing Tara back, Cat threw off the comforter and grabbed her chenille robe, slipping her feet into soft terry slippers, and went downstairs to greet them.

Throwing open the door, she was startled to see Rory standing there instead of Maureen and her daughter.

He let his eyes take in all of her. From the tousled auburn hair that hadn't seen a formal combing, to her flushed face; from the belted robe and the brushed-cotton pajamas that he could see peeking from underneath, to the ballet-like slippers that encased her slim feet.

Fresh from bed, he guessed. It didn't take much for him to imagine her tucked under the covers on this cool autumn morning; or to see himself reaching for her, pulling her body close to his. Waking her with a deep kiss, sliding his hands over and under her nightclothes, discovering the warm, supple skin below. Watching her face as she became caught up in the swirl of sensations; hearing her small cries of abandon.

He wanted her so much. Enough to throw caution to the winds and take her there.

But a cautious voice inside his head warned him that wasn't a good idea considering the circumstances, so he chose friendly conversation instead.

"Good morning." Rory held up a large brown bag,

unrolled the top so that the aroma of fresh-baked bagels wafted upward in the direction of her nose. "I brought breakfast."

"Did you now?" she asked, hands on her hips.

"You haven't eaten already, have you?" Not that he really cared. It was an excuse to see her.

"No."

"Then let me in."

"'Said the spider to the fly,'" she quoted.

One side of his mouth kicked upward. "Is that how you see me?"

Oh, he was a web master all right, Cat acknowledged as she stood there. He constructed a fine tangle of threads, woven tight and strong, layered with sensuality and charm, so that you never saw the trap coming until it closed around you.

The early-morning chill forced her hand. Cat stepped aside so that he could enter and shut the door behind him so as not to let out the warmth of her house. "Tara's not here."

"I know," he said, removing his black leather jacket and hanging it on the hall tree, making himself at home, then he followed her into the kitchen. "She called me last night."

Cat paused to look at him before continuing. "She did?"

"Yes, to tell me that I wasn't to forget her dance class this afternoon."

"She invited you to that?" Cat automatically pulled another cup from the cupboard and poured coffee for him.

"You find that strange?" He took the proffered cup, their hands briefly touching.

She grabbed another mug for herself, having left the other one upstairs on the table by her bed. "Kind of."

He shrugged as he pulled a chair out for her, then one for himself, and sat down. "Why?"

Cat wished that he would stop looking so intently at her. His blue eyes were fixed on her like a laser beam. Beneath her clothes, she felt her skin tingle, her flesh warm, her nipples tighten, her belly quiver.

What was wrong? She wasn't a green teenager, hormonally challenged. Rory Sullivan was only a man. No more, no less than any other.

Oh, who the hell was she kidding? an inner voice mocked. He was a lot more. Then. And now.

Cat took the chair that he'd pulled out for her. "It just never occurred to me that she would invite you."

Rory answered her with a smile. "I'm flattered that she did."

"Really?" Cat asked. "I can't think that attending a girl's dance class is your thing."

"And just what do you think my *thing* is?" he inquired sweetly, a twinkle in his eyes.

Seducing big girls, she wanted to say. Melting them with your charm. Catching them off guard.

"To be honest, I don't know."

"Are you sure?" he asked, one eyebrow arched.

Cat wet her lips. "Very."

"Then watching my daughter practice her steps could be very much my thing."

"Whatever." Now it was Cat's turn to shrug.

"Remember, this is all new to me."

Cat couldn't resist a moment of pride. "She's very good."

"Is she?"

"Top of her class. A real natural her instructor insists.'' Cat found she actually enjoyed sharing this information with her child's father.

"She must get that from your side of the family."

"No one in yours danced?"

"If you're referring to Irish step dancing, then no, my parents weren't the type. A sedate waltz, maybe, was their idea of dancing."

"Have you ever tried it? Step dancing, I mean."

"I've seen it performed a few times in Dublin." He took a sip of coffee. "Don't tell me that you've done it?"

Cat laughed. "I tried. So did my brother and sister. My grandmother, my mom's mom, thought it important to keep up with our heritage, so she paid for the lessons." Cat took the opportunity to take a taste of her coffee before she continued. "Didn't last long, though. I preferred reading, Kelly liked modern dance, and Brendan played baseball." Cat saw a wistful look come over Rory's face. "What?" she asked softly, curiosity getting the better of her.

"I would have liked to have played baseball."

"You didn't?"

"You don't see much of that on the Upper East Side."

"What did you play?" Rory as a little boy. What had he been like? she found herself wondering.

"Tennis."

Cat could imagine him in pristine tennis whites, racket casually slung over his shoulder, looking like an ad for the lifestyles of the well-heeled upper class. "And I'll bet that you were good at it, weren't you?"

"Reasonably so."

"What does that mean?"

"Nothing now."

Cat read something in his eyes. "But it was when you were younger, wasn't it?"

"My coach thought I could turn pro if I wanted."

She was surprised. "You were *that* good?"

"According to him."

"Did you ever think about it?"

"No, for a number of reasons."

"Your parents wouldn't have been too happy, would they?" From what little she knew of them, having a son who was a professional athlete just wasn't done. Certainly not encouraged.

"Well, let's just say that they saw tennis as a gentleman's game played at a private club, not on a touring circuit."

"But if you were that good…" She couldn't conceive of ever stopping Tara from pursuing whatever she was good at. Her parents hadn't with any of their children.

"*I* didn't want to. I enjoyed tennis, but it wasn't what I wanted to do with my life."

"And when did you know what you wanted to do?"

"When I was fourteen and my parents took me to Ireland. Getting a chance to see history up close made it so real for me. It fascinated me as nothing had before." And almost nothing since, he wanted to add. Until he met an auburn-haired bookstore owner who was a welcome breath of fresh air into his stale life. "It was like a dangerous drug," he explained, "leaving me craving more."

Cat could well understand that—he'd been the same for her, until she'd stopped, cold turkey. "Would you like something to eat?" She was getting hungry and couldn't very well fix breakfast for herself and ignore him. Not that there was much chance of anyone in their right mind ever ignoring Rory Sullivan, especially if that someone was a woman.

"Do you have any genuine Irish oatmeal?"

"Sorry," she replied. "Just the one-minute kind, why?"

"I was recalling breakfasts in Ireland on a day like today. Thick oatmeal, freshly made, hot and laden with cream."

Cat almost choked on her coffee, managing to just barely swallow it after that remark. Only Rory, she thought, could make a description of oatmeal sound erotic.

She rose from her chair and pulled a large cardboard container from inside a glass-enclosed cabinet. "Will this do?"

"Sure."

She bent down and retrieved a heavy aluminum saucepan from a cabinet below.

Rory offered, "Can I help?"

"Why don't you put the bagels in the toaster? There's jam in the fridge."

She handed him a long, sharp knife to slice the bagels open, watching out of the corner of her eye as he efficiently set about his task, moving with grace around her kitchen. In no time he had the bagels toasting, several assorted jams lined up on the table; brought out the cream and found a small cut-glass pitcher to place it in. He gave a good impression of being domesticated. But that's probably all it was. An impression. A show. Put on to confuse her. Make her think that he was tame, when in reality he was anything but.

Rory watched as she stirred the pot, oddly excited by her domesticity. For him, it was something outside the ordinary. A preview of what could be. What *should* be if he had anything to say about it. And he would. By whatever means.

If Cat thought it odd that she was cooking breakfast for a man who two months ago she hadn't thought she'd ever see again, she kept it to herself. The improbability of the situation brought a smile to her lips. It was almost as if they were an old married couple.

Except that they weren't.

What was she thinking? he wondered as she spooned out the oatmeal into bowls, placing them on the table, along with a sealed glass jar that held dark brown sugar, and he buttered the bagels, piling them into a medium-sized china plate.

They both sat down and began to eat, each maintaining their own counsel until Rory broke the silence.

"We should tell Tara the truth."

"You mean that I should, don't you?" Cat asked, fixing her glance on him.

"No, I think we should both tell her, together."

"I don't know if she's ready."

"That's a chance we'll have to take."

She paused in the act of applying a thick layer of strawberry jam to her bagel. "Why?"

"Because we can't go on as we are."

"What's wrong with doing just that?"

"It's not fair to her, or to us."

"That's your opinion, Rory."

'Granted, it is. But it's an honest one."

"And you think I'm not being honest?"

"Are you?"

"What's that supposed to mean?"

"I think you know."

"If I did, I wouldn't be asking," she countered, laying down her knife.

''Yes, you would. To throw me off.''

''Off what? The nearest tall building?''

He smiled. ''The scent.''

'What the hell are you talking about, Rory?''

''Don't pretend to be obtuse. ''

''It's no pretense. I really don't know what you're talking about.''

He looked at her face, studied her eyes. She was as aware as he was of the chemistry between them, even if she was pretending that she wasn't. And maybe that was a good thing. Something that could work to his advantage.

He took a deep breath. ''We've gotten off track. We should tell Tara, and soon.''

''She's just getting used to you. This might confuse her.''

''And it might clear things up, too,'' he pointed out.

''Let me see.''

''You can't keep putting this off, Cat.''

''What's the rush?''

''I want to provide for my daughter.''

''You can do that without her finding out the truth.''

''I can, but I don't want to.''

''Does she mean that much to you?''

Rory's face grew thoughtful. ''Funnily enough, yes. I didn't know, to be honest, when I first met her if she would. It wasn't as if I had nine months to get used to the idea. She was there. A person in her own right.''

A loving smile curved Cat's mouth. ''She's certainly that.''

''But half of her is me, a Sullivan, and I want everyone to know that, most especially I want my daughter to know that. There's no walking away from her now. Morally, or legally.''

Cat's eyes widened. "What do you mean, legally? Have you hired an attorney?"

"I've sought out legal advice, yes."

"And what did they tell you?"

"That as her father I'm entitled to certain rights."

"Such as?" Cat was beginning to feel afraid, cornered.

"Visitation, at the very least."

"I haven't stopped you, have I?"

"No. But suppose that I wanted to take her somewhere without you? I don't have a legal right to do that." He paused, then added, "Yet."

"Take her? Where?"

"Anywhere. New York. Ireland. To the movies, a show."

"You're talking about a custody suit?" She got up from her chair, pacing a few steps away.

"If I have to."

Cat tried to keep her voice level, when what she really wanted to do was scream. "You'd do that to her?"

"I don't want to. It's all up to you."

"Me?"

"Yes. Marry me and we could both raise our daughter. Then there'd be no need to have the courts involved. Any legal matters could be seen to privately. Discreetly."

"And if I don't?"

"I think you can guess."

She could. He had enough money to back up his implied threat, and they both knew it. "You're not giving me much of a choice in the matter, are you?"

"You always have a choice, Cat. You know that better than anyone." Rory knew what she thought—that he would fight her in a long, drawn-out battle if she didn't agree. What she didn't know was that this was a gamble. He'd never do that to her, or to their child. But he had to let her think that he would. Especially if that was the only way he could get her to say yes, to agree to marry him. After the ceremony, after he found a way to make her love him again, then he would tell her the truth. That it was all a wild risk that he was willing to take. Had to take. For all their sakes.

"I need your answer."

Cat suddenly felt as if her life was spiraling out of control. That she was trapped in some bizarre parallel universe. "I really don't think that you've quite thought this out, Rory."

"Oh, but I have. Very thoroughly, I can assure you."

"What about love?"

"I loved you once," he said, his voice low and seductively sweet, "and that wasn't exactly a success, for either of us."

"Maybe because we had different ideas of what love was."

"That's the past, and I'm interested in the future," he stressed.

"Are you?" she asked. "Or do you still want things your own way?"

"We both do, don't we?" he countered. "So what's your answer?"

Cat took a deep breath, exhaling slowly. "What do you think?"

"Tell me."

"Yes."

"Good." The gamble had paid off.

"But," she added, "with a few conditions."

"Such as?"

"We don't tell Tara about you until she's had a chance to get used to this change first."

"You're suggesting that I postpone telling her that I'm her father?"

Cat nodded. "I think it would be for the best. Give her time to adjust."

"All right." He could see she had a valid point. "What else?"

"I want you to give me time to get used to it, too."

"Delay being your husband in fact as well as on paper?"

"Yes."

Rory fixed his eyes on hers. "For how long?"

"As long as it takes."

"That's unacceptable."

Cat's face paled. She wasn't ready for the kind of intimacy he wanted. "You can't expect me to jump into your bed right away? As if this were truly a love match."

"Perhaps not. But we will share one."

"What are you talking about?"

Rory explained. "I don't intend to sleep alone, Cat, or on a couch, or in another room. All that will do is keep us strangers to one another."

"And you propose…?"

"We share a bedroom as well as a home."

"I have no intentions of moving my daughter from this house," she stated emphatically. "She'll have enough to cope with."

"We all will. And no, I wouldn't want you to uproot her. Since I'm only renting the town house, I'll move in with you. Is your bed big enough for both of us?"

Cat couldn't help it, color flooded her cheeks at his suggestion because it stirred up thoughts of her daydreams while reading the book earlier. There, in her fantasy, she could control the situation, be in complete charge, because it was just that—a fantasy, nothing more. He wanted reality, and reality could be dangerous, both for her body and soul. "It's a queen."

"Good. I was never one for doubles if I had a choice."

The bed they'd first made love in was a double, as she recalled. A very intimate space that had served them well.

"Anything else?"

"You let me tell my family and Tara."

"Agreed. Now, I've one or two conditions of my own."

"And they would be?" What else could he want? she wondered.

"That we get married soon."

"How soon?"

"Within the next few weeks."

"A civil ceremony?" It was probably for the best. Did it really matter to her that whenever she dreamt about a wedding ceremony, it was something warm and inviting, filled with friends and family? Not a rushed appointment with a let's-get-this-show-going-as-I've-got-others-to-do-too judge.

"A cold, quick affair at city hall?" he asked. "No." He repeated his denial. "No way I want something like that, for either of us, or for our daughter to witness. Let me handle the details. I'll see to it that it's memorable." Rory stood up, stepped over to where she stood, her back to the counter, his hands lightly clasping her arms. "You won't regret this, Cat. I promise." He let go of one arm to move his hand to cup her chin, lifting it. He bent his head and touched his mouth to hers, kissing her softly, lingering long enough to create an impression, and a promise.

"Let's have dinner tonight."

Recovering, Cat inhaled, her tongue snaking out to wet her lips. "It's not necessary."

"It is for me. We have one more piece of business to take care of."

"What would that be?"

"Tonight. You'll get the answer then."

"Are you going to wait for Tara?" She wanted him to leave so that she could be alone, collect her thoughts.

"No. I'll see you later at her dance class." Rory skimmed his index finger along her cheek. "It'll be for the best, Cat. Trust me."

"That's asking a lot."

"I know," he said, wanting desperately to tell her the truth of his feelings, but realizing that now wasn't the time. "But try. If not for your sake, then for our daughter's."

"You'll see to everything then?" Rory asked the wedding planner less than an hour later.

The perky blonde gave him her best and most dazzling smile. "Normally, this short of a lead time wouldn't have worked for me, but since you know exactly what you want, and are willing to pay for it, there should be no problem. Are you sure that your bride-to-be doesn't want to add anything to your list?"

Rory smiled. "She's leaving it all up to me."

The woman checked her handwritten list once more, quickly going through the check marks she made. "Well, I think you've got everything covered. And I love the theme and the colors you've picked out. I'm impressed. Especially since most of the grooms I deal with are just as happy to let their future wives handle everything." She smiled again. "You must love her very much."

"More than you can ever guess," he replied. "And more than she'll ever know."

"How utterly romantic. Why is it," she asked in a deep, sighing voice, "that all the good ones are taken?" She shot a look at her assistant, a handsome young man, at the other end of the office, who was on the phone with another client. "Or gay?" She chuckled. "Well, she'll be so thrilled when it all comes together. What woman wouldn't be with something as romantic as what you've got here?"

"That's the idea."

"It's great working with people who know what they want. Spare me from the oh-I'm-not-sures and the well-let-me-think-about-thats."

"I didn't always," Rory confessed, charming her with a lazy smile, bedroom eyes and sexy voice. "But I do now, and that's what's important."

She glanced at her list again. "Oh, you've left off the honeymoon destination? Do you want me to find something for you?"

"I have that taken care of."

"Do you mind my asking where?"

"Back to where it began."

There was a quizzical look on her face. "Pardon?"

Rory laughed. "It's a private joke, Miss Baker."

"Okay." She put down her pencil. "I'm sure it'll be perfect."

"I'm not really concerned with perfect," he said. "Just memorable." Rory got up from the plush leather chair and shook her hand. "I'll expect to hear from you by Monday."

"Fine. I'll start making calls and sending faxes right away. I should have everything squared away by then." Ashley Baker extended her hand. "Your fiancée is one lucky lady, Mr. Sullivan."

Rory took her hand, absently comparing it to Cat's. Miss Baker's nails were long and tapered, painted a dark shade of crimson, which matched her power suit. Cat's were shorter, glossed in a sheer shade. There was no question in his mind whose nails he'd want clinging to his bare back, making their mark. "You've got that all wrong, Miss Baker. I'm the lucky one."

Cat was making up her bed, when, in the act of smoothing the floral sheet back into place, her glance fell to the width of the bed.

Rory. He made it quite plain that he intended to share this bed with her. His body next to hers. His clothes in her walk-in closet. His stuff in her bathroom. His body in her tub.

She picked up one of the pillows, fluffing it. Another head, his, would leave its mark. Another scent, masculine, would be captured by the pillowcase.

God, why had she agreed to this farce?

Because she had no other choice.

In a few weeks she'd be a bride. A Mrs. A wife. Sharing her home, her life, her bed, and her daughter.

Cat hugged the pillow to her chest, a solitary tear cascaded down her cheek.

If only...

But she couldn't live her life on if onlys.

She had to live it in the here and now. Had to find a

way to tell her daughter that their family would be expanding to include Rory Sullivan.

Brushing away the tear, Cat replaced the pillow and went to get dressed.

Chapter Nine

"Tara, I have something to talk to you about," Cat said as she and the little girl entered the house later that day.

"What is it, Mommy?" Tara asked as she pulled off her jean jacket and tossed it over the newel post.

"First off," Cat announced, "I want you to hang your coat up in the closet."

"Okay." Tara did as she was told, then followed her mother into the den.

"Sit right here, honey," Cat said, making room on the sofa for Tara to join her.

The little girl hopped up and went right to her mother's side, burrowing against Cat's body.

Cat held her daughter close, smoothing back the long dark hair that had come loose from its braid. "You like Mr. Sullivan, don't you?"

"An awful lot," Tara replied. "That's why I asked

him to come and see me dance, Mommy. It was nice having him there. And I'd like it if he came when I had soccer practice too.''

''Would you like it if he were around more often?''

The little girl pulled back just a bit so that she could see her mother's face. ''What do you mean?''

''Would you like it if Mr. Sullivan was here on a more permanent basis with us?''

Tara's blue eyes lit up. ''Is he gonna move in? Joe's dad has a girl who just moved in with him.''

''No, this would be a bit different,'' Cat explained, not wanting to get into the complicated issue of a man and woman just living together. ''Mr. Sullivan wants to marry me.''

Tara's head tilted, as if she was considering a weighty issue. ''Would that make him my daddy?''

Cat expelled a deep breath. ''Yes, honey. He'd be Mommy's husband and your new father.''

The little girl pondered her mother's words. ''So, he'd sleep over all the time?''

''Uh-huh.''

''And he could help me with my homework, too?''

''Yes.''

Tara was growing more and more enthusiastic. ''And we could go riding again?''

''Certainly.''

''Do you like him, Mommy?''

Like? She felt a lot of things for Rory Sullivan. She didn't know if like was, or ever would be, part of the package. ''I wouldn't be considering his proposal if I didn't, sweetheart.'' God forgive me this little white lie, she prayed.

''Then I guess that it's okay.''

Cat hugged her daughter close, hoping that she was doing the right thing.

"Is he moving in right away?"

"No, darling. He and Mommy have to get married first."

"Oh, do you get to wear a white dress?"

Cat's lips curved into a grin. "I'll see."

"And do we get to have a party?"

"A small one, I think."

"Do I get to get dressed up?"

"Oh yes," Cat said. "We can go out and look for something special for you this coming week, if you'd like."

Tara nodded her head.

Cat ran a hand nervously through her hair. "You really are happy about this, aren't you?"

"Oh yeah, Mommy," Tara said enthusiastically. "I can't wait to tell my friends at school. This is almost as good as getting a dog."

Her daughter's answer brought another smile to Cat's mouth. She and Tara had had this conversation before. Tara wanted a puppy and Cat had always said, "When you're older." Every few months Tara would ask if she was older yet so that she could get a puppy.

"Though," Tara added, her eyes brimming with delight, "I still would like a puppy."

"We'll talk about that later, honey," Cat said. "Now, why don't you go upstairs and take off your dance clothes, then you can have a cup of hot chocolate? Would you like that?"

Tara nodded.

"And I've got another surprise for you."

"What?"

"Lindsey is coming over to baby-sit you tonight."

"How come?"

"Mommy's going out tonight with Mr. Sullivan. He's taking me to dinner."

"For pizza?" Tara's eyes lit up at the prospect.

"No," Cat chuckled. "We're going to a regular restaurant, sweetheart." She didn't know where Rory was planning on taking her; he'd only said that it was someplace fancy and for her to wear something special. "But, you can order pizza when Lindsey gets here, how about that?" Cat held up her hand, palm toward her daughter.

"Cool." Tara slapped her own hand against her mother's in a high-five.

"Okay. Then why don't you go and get changed, I'll bring up your hot chocolate, and then you help me pick out a dress to wear tonight."

Tara smiled her acceptance and bolted for the stairs.

Cat was happy that Tara wasn't upset about the change in their lives that was going to occur. It was probably due to Rory's charm, which he dispensed freely, because Tara obviously had begun to adore him.

Now, if only she could get as enthused about this change in their life.

Walking upstairs a few minutes later, Cat found her daughter going through her closet.

"Here's your hot chocolate, Tara. Careful you don't spill it."

Tara emerged from the walk-in closet and took the oversized mug from her mother. "I won't, Mommy."

"Good." Cat glanced into the open doorway. "Did you find anything?"

"There are two that are really pretty."

"Which ones?"

"The bluish-green and the dark brown."

Cat walked inside and spotted the two dresses. One

as a turquoise jersey and the other was a chocolate-brown velvet jumper that she wore with a very fancy lace white blouse. She looked each one over carefully before she made her decision, then pulled it off the rack to show Tara. "This one, I think."

Tara nodded happily.

"Good. Now it's time for my bath."

"Can I add the beads?"

Tara got a kick out of the various packets of scent that Cat added to her bathwater. "Certainly."

Tara placed her mug on the nightstand and ran into her mother's bathroom, grabbing the decorated paper packet from several that filled a woven basket.

Cat followed her in, turned on the taps, and adjusted the temperature. "What did you choose?" she asked, clipping her hair onto the top of her head.

"This one!" Tara exclaimed as she handed it to her mother. "It's my favorite."

Cat tore open the packet, sniffing appreciatively, then letting her daughter do the same before she added the beads to the warm water. "Mine too."

The scent to lilies of the valley permeated the room as the concentrated perfume in the beads was released upon impact with the water.

"I'll bet Mr. Sullivan will like it too, Mommy," Tara opined.

Would he notice? Cat wondered as she sank into the tub, her clothes dumped in a heap on the floor as Tara left her to watch TV. Who was she kidding? Of course he would notice. That was one thing that hadn't changed about him. He was always cognizant of what a woman wore, how she smelled, every little thing about her. And because he was, Rory made a woman that much more aware of being female.

In a matter of weeks they would be sharing this bathroom. He would be able to walk in on her at any time. Look his fill. Touch?

Cat closed her eyes as she ran the sponge-cloth over her body, down her arms, over her breasts, across her thighs. All of a sudden it took on a life of its own and another hand, a masculine hand, was guiding it. Rubbing the textured item across her skin, around her neck, between her legs.

Cat's eyes flew open quickly.

That was enough of that! She didn't need any help from him in taking her bath. Besides, there was a lock on the door. All she had to do was make sure that it was turned when she wanted her privacy. Even Rory wouldn't force the issue then. That wasn't his style.

She hoped.

Rory smoothed his favorite aftershave along his freshly shaved cheeks and over his jaw. Tonight was special. He'd called ahead to the restaurant and ordered the dinner, the wine and the dessert. He wanted everything perfect, which is why he booked a private room, made arrangements for what flowers would grace the table.

He walked into his dressing room, picking out his clothes with care. Satisfied with his selection, he dropped the towel that clung to his hips and proceeded to dress.

When he was finished, he checked his look in the mirror that hung over the bureau. A few adjustments and he was ready.

He reached out and picked up the small velvet box that lay there. Opening it, he smiled as he gazed upon the ring inside. It was exquisite. And on Cat's finger, it would complement her beauty. Yes, it would suit her well. No modern, cold jewel and setting for her. She deserved the best. Something with class, elegance, and made by a true craftsman, one who recognized the unique. This ring had it all.

Somehow he doubted that Cat would be expecting anything this grand. And that would be half the fun— seeing her reaction to the ring when he presented it to her.

It should also satisfy anyone's curiosity about their forthcoming nuptials. A man didn't give this kind of ring to a partner in a business arrangement. This was a ring that spoke *commitment*. It stated this was a treasure for a treasure. It represented, rightly so, all the things that Rory wanted to say and couldn't. Not yet. Cat wasn't ready to listen. Or believe. She would probably see it as a stamp of possession, or a flaunting of his considerable wealth. He saw it instead as a proclamation, a statement of love renewed.

Maybe after they'd had a chance to get to know one another again, as a man and woman should, without barriers, without restrictions, without interference, then she would understand and accept it in the true spirit that it was offered. Perhaps then he could show her what he really felt. Discover if the sexual sparks that he sensed still existed between them could be fanned into the worthy flames of deep and abiding love again.

"Would you get that, Lindsey? I'm not ready yet," Cat called down the stairs as the front-door bell rang.

"Sure thing, Ms. Kildare," the young girl answered, adjusting the level of sound on the TV, set to her favorite video channel.

She opened the door, and her jaw dropped. Standing there was a movie-star handsome dude. Recalling the average looks of the two other men her neighbor had dated this past year, Lindsey mentally decided that Ms. Kildare's taste was vastly improving.

She gave the stranger a wide smile. "You must be Mr. Sullivan. Ms. Kildare said you were nice-looking, but that doesn't cover it," Lindsey declared candidly. "Come on in. She's still upstairs getting ready."

Rory stepped inside, aware of the young girl's wide, appreciative eyes. He smiled and asked, "And you are?"

"Lindsey Reynolds, Tara's baby-sitter." She narrowed her eyes, staring intently at him.

Rory put out his hand. "So lovely to meet you. And have you been seeing to Tara for long?" This young girl saw the resemblance, he realized, between himself and his daughter; he could readily read it on her face. Would she make a comment?—or let it pass?

"Ever since Ms. Kildare moved in here the year before last."

Rory remained cool. "And you're prepared to stay late, in case we are?"

"Sure," the teenager answered. "No sweat. I only live down the street, so it's no big deal. You know you look an awfully lot like—"

"Rory," Tara yelled as she flew down the steps and was caught up in Rory's arms. "Mommy told me the news."

He hugged her close, one hand touching her head, wondering where all this heretofore untapped love for this little girl that grew deeper each day sprang from. "Were you pleased?"

"Uh-huh," the little girl responded. "I think it's neat."

"Neat, eh?"

"Sure." She kissed his cheek. "Mmm," she said. "You smell good. Just as good as Mommy."

"Thanks, my lady fair."

Tara giggled. "Mommy said to tell you that she'll be down in just a minute."

"Then why don't we wait for her in the den?" he asked, putting Tara down.

The little girl took hold of his hand. "He's gonna be my daddy soon," she announced to the baby-sitter.

The teenager's clever eyes widened. "You don't say?"

"Uh-huh," Tara responded. "He and my mommy are gonna get married."

"Cool." Lindsey followed them into the room, grabbing the remote and turning the sound down even further. "That's nice." She flopped down on the other end of the sofa. "What do you do, Mr. Sullivan? Are you a model or something?"

"Nothing quite so glamorous, I can assure you," he said. "I teach at the university."

"And he writes books," Tara chimed in, beaming at her new father-to-be.

"Like Stephen King?" the girl asked. "He's my favorite."

Rory shook his head. "I'm afraid not." He saw the interest fade from the teenager's eyes. "History is what I do."

"History?"

"Yes."

"Oh."

Rory almost laughed at the blatant disappointment in the perky teenager's tone. "Not your favorite subject, I take it?"

"Not hardly," she responded with a dramatic roll of

her eyes. "All that stuff about dead people and things that don't exist anymore. I'm more interested in the future."

"Such as?"

"Designing Web sites. I did Ms. Kildare's for the bookstore."

"Then I'm impressed," Rory said. "It's quite good."

The teenager beamed. "I got extra credit for my advanced computer class for that. Mr. Heller was impressed too."

"Maybe I should talk to you about setting up one for me? I've been told that it's something I should seriously consider."

"Sure, I could do that," the girl promised, her tone liquid and soft. "Just let me know what you need."

"Trying to lure away the baby-sitter, Rory?" Cat asked, standing in the doorway.

He stood up, his eyes taking an inventory of her. God, but every time he thought Cat couldn't get any more stunning, she surprised him. Gone was the casual look she'd worn that afternoon, jeans and a sweater set. It was replaced by a formfitting V-necked velvet jumper in deepest brown that ended a few inches above the knee. Underneath the dress was an antique Edwardian lace blouse in white. Her glorious red hair was piled on her head, with tendrils escaping, framing her face.

Damn, but he still craved her with an unquenchable, ever-growing hunger. And, Rory promised himself right then, he would have her. Theirs was a prickly war of wills, a battle of equals which neither could lose.

He thought about the brooch he'd purchased in Ireland and which was safely tucked away in his safe-deposit box at the bank. The old gold would have set off her outfit to perfection. Just this afternoon he'd decided to give it to her as a wedding present.

Cat's breath momentarily caught in her throat. He looked handsome beyond compare, and she couldn't resist a small smile that curved her lips. He'd also chosen brown. Well, sort of. His wool suit was a plaid blend of soft gray and camel that outlined his broad shoulders and lean frame. A matching vest with an antique gold pocket watch and crisp white linen shirt and gray silk tie completed the ensemble. Already her hands itched to smooth over the fabric, to get a tactile sense of him.

No man had the right to be that devastatingly attractive. It wasn't fair. Not when she wanted to keep her distance from him once they were wed.

But it was just her body that was reacting so traitorously to him, she told herself. Her heart wasn't involved. It was only a chemical response she was powerless to control. Female hormones responded to the masculine, acting on instinct alone.

"Quite the contrary, my dear," Rory drawled. "I'm more than willing to share. Miss Reynolds has offered her expert computer services to me."

"Oh, she has?" It wasn't hard for Cat to read the look of sheer fascination on her baby-sitter's face. How many of his students gazed at him like that—as if he'd hung the moon? How many went further? Offered themselves, eager to discover the secrets that were hidden behind his dark blue eyes? Or the ones to be found in his embrace? And what about faculty? Was he even now sharing time with someone else? Sharing bed, body, heart?

God, she sounded like a jealous twit. It wasn't that. Of course not, she declared silently. It was only that once they were married, she'd be damned if he would humiliate her by carrying on with another woman. No, by God. If she had to give up her freedom for this sham of a marriage, then so would he. She'd make that clear to him. Playing a wife was one thing; playing a fool was quite another.

"You're very lucky then, she's very good at making sense of the intricacies of the Internet." Cat turned her attention to the younger girl. "You have my cell phone number, right?"

The girl rattled off a number. "No problem."

Cat smiled. "We shouldn't be too late."

"Mr. Sullivan told me that you might be, so that's no problem," Lindsey said, giving her employer a wink. "Go out and have a blast."

Cat shot a penetrating glance at Rory, as if to question his words to the baby-sitter.

"I suggest that we go," he said, not taking the bait. "I have reservations for eight-thirty."

"Where?" Cat inquired, wanting to let the baby-sitter know where she would be.

"Seasons."

He named the most exclusive eating establishment in the county. Its reputation was well deserved, or so she'd been told by her brother, but it was always booked weeks in advance because it was small, holding not more than thirty people at a time. She should have guessed if anyone could secure reservations at that place, it would be him. Charm and money were really a potent combination. Charm, money and sex appeal could be deadly.

He caught the surprised look on her face. "It's just a restaurant, Cat," he said as he moved closer to her. "Do you have a coat?"

"Saying that Seasons is just a restaurant is tantamount to saying *Les Miserables* is a moderately successful musical,'' she countered. ''And yes, I do. It's in the hall closet. Gray wool.''

''Then let's get it and be on our way.''

Cat ignored him for the moment and bent down, holding out her arms so that Tara could run into them. She kissed her daughter and hugged her close. ''Be good and mind Lindsey. Okay?''

''I will, Mommy,'' Tara promised.

Rory appeared in the doorway, her coat in his hands. ''Cat,'' he called softly.

She got up and turned. ''Coming.''

You will be if I have any say in the matter, Rory thought as he held out the coat, into which Cat slipped her arms. For the rest of our lives together.

She pulled the belt tight on the wraparound trenchcoat style. ''I'm ready.'' As I'll ever be, she added mentally.

''Rory,'' came the plaintive cry of his daughter.

He stood there as the little girl hurled herself at him, catching him about the legs. ''Take good care of my mommy,'' she said, tilting her head back and looking way up to him.

''I will, my lady fair,'' he promised, bending to place a kiss on the top of her head. ''Always. My word to you.''

When they were in Rory's car, Cat said, ''Don't make promises to Tara that you may not keep.''

He slanted her a quick look before he returned his focus to the road ahead. ''Who said I wasn't going to keep my word to her?''

''She's a child, Rory. One who takes things to heart.''

''I can see that for myself.''

''If you can, then you should know that she believes what you tell her.''

"I'm glad that she does."

"Then know she'll expect you to keep your word."

"I intend to, Cat."

"To take good care of me?" She gave a short snort of disbelief.

"That's what's implied in marriage, isn't it? That we'll both take care of the other? And of our child? Or children?"

Cat was taken aback by his seemingly genuine response, delivered in a most sincere tone. "Yes." Then her mind focused on the plural word he used. "Children?"

"I don't think I'd like Tara to be an only child. Do you?"

"I can't think about that now," she pleaded, because that led to thinking about how one conceived a child, and those images were just too erotic to contemplate right then.

The same images were leapfrogging through Rory's brain, forcing him to concentrate on his driving before he was tempted to pull the car off the road and put them into play for real. Luckily for both of them, the restaurant was dead ahead.

"Welcome to Seasons, madam," the doorman chimed in as he helped her from the car while a valet took the keys from Rory's hand. "You *do* have a reservation?"

"Sullivan," Rory said.

The doorman consulted his list. "Yes, here it is. Party of two. Private dining room. Down the hall and first door to the right, sir." He unlocked the double-arched wooden doors and let them in. "Have a wonderful evening."

Cat almost burst into laughter as they went through the heavy door to the interior, the dark-paneled walls fitted with sconces. The place reminded her of an English manor home, and was furnished as such, with hunting prints of horses and dogs, furniture that complemented the authentic decor. "I half expected that we were going to be fingerprinted to see if we were who you said," she murmured to Rory.

He joined in her lightheartedness. "Maybe that's later."

A woman in her mid-thirties walked down the hall to greet them. "Welcome to Seasons, Miss Kildare, Mr. Sullivan. May I take your coats?"

Rory helped Cat remove hers before he took off his topcoat, which the woman placed in a nearby huge pine armoire.

Cat didn't even question how the woman knew who they were.

"The room you requested is ready, sir, if you would be so good as to follow me."

Rory took Cat's arm, and they both followed the woman the few short steps to the private dining room.

Instead of dark paneling, the walls were painted a rich, deep warm red, hung with Regency era portraits.

Cat noticed the silver bucket next to the small, intimate mahogany dining table. Champagne was already chilling. Two fluted glasses were set, waiting to be filled with the bubbly liquid.

"Would you like me to open it, sir, or would your rather do that yourself?"

"I can manage quite well," Rory assured the woman.

"Then I'll leave you to it. Your appetizers will be along in just a few minutes."

"Thank you."

When the door was shut, leaving them alone, Cat asked, "You ordered already?"

"I took the liberty." He picked up the bottle and proceeded to remove the cork swiftly and efficiently, pouring them both a glass. "I hope that you don't mind?"

"And if I said I did?" Cat questioned as she accepted the glass.

"Then I'd see that you got whatever it is you wanted."

Why was it that when he said that, her wayward thoughts weren't on food?

"But you'll like what I ordered." He took a sip of the champagne, pleased that it was the vintage he'd requested. "Promise." His mouth curved into a smile. "Now, let us have a toast."

"To what?"

"Why, to us, of course," he replied smoothly. Rory clinked his glass against hers, the peal of crystal hitting crystal the only sound as they both drank to his salutation.

Chapter Ten

He was right, damn him. She did love what he chose. Everything was perfect, and no detail was overlooked, from the sumptuous crab bisque to the grilled salmon steaks. Dessert was a surprise too. No ordinary fare like cake or pie. The waiter had wheeled in a stainless-steel trolley draped with antique linen. On the trolley were several china plates filled with assorted cheese and fruits. A bottle of vintage port was also produced and shown to Rory for his approval.

He nodded and the waiter laid out the selections, then discreetly vanished.

It was almost as though he really cared about her comforts, her likes. As if he hadn't cleverly and calculatingly blackmailed her into this relationship. As if there was still an emotional spark left from their former time together.

"Try the farmhouse cheddar," Rory suggested with a

smile that revealed his perfect teeth. "It's got quite a lovely taste." He took the silver cheese cutter and removed a sliver for her, picking it up with his fingers and holding it out to her.

She knew what he wanted—for her to nip the cheese from his outstretched fingers with her mouth.

Instead, she gingerly lifted it with her own fingertips, enjoying the sample. "Another slice, please," she requested, "but this time, make it bigger."

Was it his imagination, or had she emphasized the last word?

Cat picked a few of the fruits and put them on a small plate, handed them to Rory, then accepted the plate he'd made up for her with several of the cheeses represented.

She tried each one, gave him her opinion, then settled in to sample voraciously from the fruit platter as well.

He watched her for a few minutes before asking, "A penny for them."

"What?"

"Your thoughts," Rory replied, sipping his glass of port. "You looked so far away just now."

"Actually," she admitted freely, "I was right here."

"Thinking…?"

"You honestly want to know?"

He nodded. "Of course."

"Why you went to all this trouble for me."

"It was no trouble," he said smoothly.

"You know what I mean." She waved her hand, indicating the table, their meal. "It's all so wonderful. Anyone would think we *were* a happy couple."

"And you don't think that's possible?"

She turned the question around to him. "Do you?"

His rapid-fire response surprised her. "Yes."

"Really?"

"Why not?" he inquired. "We were, once. We could be again if we both worked at it."

"You sound so certain."

"I am."

Confidence or arrogance? she wondered. "I'm not so sure."

"Is that because you don't want to be happy?"

"That's ridiculous," she immediately retorted. "Of course I want to be happy. I was."

"Until I came back?" he asked softly.

"You said that, not me."

"But that's what you think, isn't it?"

"I don't know how to answer that."

"Yes, you do."

"Then you're right," she said, taking her cue from him. "I *was* happy."

"There's nothing stopping you from being that way again, you know."

She gave him an arch look. "Isn't there?"

"Only yourself, Cat."

"You don't think you're a factor?"

He shrugged. "Maybe."

"There's no maybe about it, Rory."

"If I am," he responded, "then I'll do whatever I can to ensure that fact."

"By *making* me marry you?"

"By making sure that you're never sorry that you said yes. Even if it was only for our daughter's sake."

It sounded so simple when he explained it that way, but Cat knew that nothing was ever simple with Rory. Their union would be fraught with emotional quicksand, surrounded by lacerated dreams. What kind of a foundation was that?

The best that she could hope for right now, she supposed.

Rory reached into his suit jacket's interior pocket, pulling an object from it. Then he leaned over the table and gently lifted Cat's left hand. "This is to make it official."

He'd bought her a ring. Well, she guessed that he would have to if he wanted people to think that this was a regular engagement. A nice diamond, discreet and perfect, she assumed by the Fortunoff name on the box.

He slipped it on her finger, and Cat took a good look at it.

The breath caught in her throat in an audible gasp. Far from being the typical ring she expected, this was a ring that brought another era to mind. An era of romance, of stolen kisses and damn-the-consequences love.

"Do you like it?"

Cat held out her hand, admiring the way the stone caught the light from the chandelier and the wall sconces, and how it looked on her finger. As if it *belonged*. As if it had been waiting for her. Silly, she knew, but she couldn't help it. Her rapport with this particular piece of jewelry was instantaneous.

"Oh yes," she said softly, in awe. "It's magnificent." Just when she thought she had Rory figured out, he did something like this. Confounded her. Shocked her.

"When I saw it, it reminded me of you."

"How so?" She couldn't take her eyes from it as light sparkled in its depths, bouncing off the center stone.

"The color. It was pure, full of life. Cool one minute, intensely warm the next. Like—" Rory paused for effect ""—your eyes."

A shot of heat speared through her, hitting her square in the stomach.

"It's got a history."

"I thought it might."

"It was the property of a lady," he explained, "given to her by her lover, who, I was told, waited patiently for his beloved to be free to come to him so that they could wed."

"How wildly romantic."

Yes, he thought, *isn't it? I can wait, too, Cat. As long as it takes.*

"And did she?"

"What do you think?"

Cat dropped her eyes to the ring again. "She did. Later maybe than he expected, but she didn't forget what they had shared, what they would share again."

As will we, Cat. I'm sure of it.

"Dance with me," he suddenly whispered, his voice compelling her to pay attention.

Cat looked up. She was so caught up in the moment that she hadn't noticed that the background music coming from the speakers had changed. Gone was the soft sound of classical music; it was replaced by music she recognized—one of her favorite male singers, whose powerful renditions of love songs had always melted her heart.

God, one more thing he remembered about her.

Cat went into Rory's arms with a sense of ineluctability.

He could read her face so clearly, recognize the glow that lit her eyes. Slowly. Surely. Eventually. He had to believe that. Had to keep telling himself that he would succeed. There was too much at stake for him to lose.

She fit so right, so perfect in his embrace. Rory recalled another time when they had danced like this. It was the day after they had first made love. She had been in the kitchen, wearing a shorty robe, humming to herself to a song on the radio. He came up behind her and whirled her into his arms, and they danced, giddy with their love.

Now it was different. Now it was a dance of familiar strangers, poised on the edge of remembrance and renewal. He could feel the movement of her body against his as he tightened his hold, swaying in time to the music.

Cat felt the imprint of Rory's hand on her back, warming her skin even through the velvet of the dress that she wore. His splayed fingers pressed her closer to the heat and strength of his taut thighs.

Rory was conscious of the effect she had on him, as he was aware of the impact his actions had on her. He could feel the delicate tremblings in her body communicate themselves to him, resonating with a corresponding need in him. Having Caitlyn here, now, was all that was important. Capturing, if only for a short while, the elusive threads of what once was. Reaching past the shadows and following the light of what could be.

There was no surprise when his lips finally touched hers. They were warm, mobile, persuasive. Cat willingly opened her mouth to the probing demand of his tongue, matching it, the rustiness of the action fading as impulse and instinct took over. Somehow, her hands were on his back, under the jacket, capturing the feel of the smooth, crisp shirt beneath her eager, exploring fingers.

She heard a moan, low and acute. It was her own voice, she discovered when his mouth left hers. His lips continued to plunder, to stimulate as they nibbled on her earlobe, licking and tugging the soft skin. Then Rory found the vulnerable spot on her neck, exposed by her upswept hair.

Involuntarily, Cat's hand reached out to stroke his cheek; his face turned to her caress, reminding her of a cat having its fur petted as he rubbed against her palm. Not an ordinary cat, she thought; never a tame house animal. No, he was a sleek, magnificent beast allowing this contact, instinctly craving it, forcing her somehow to act upon the unspoken.

Rory was doing it to her again, she realized. The potent force of his charm was turning her, catching her off balance, spinning her away from her purpose.

When he would have taken her mouth once more, she pulled back, her arms falling to her sides.

In a voice that she managed to make sound calm with the greatest of efforts, Cat said slowly, enunciating each word, "Take me home."

Rory struggled to get his breathing back to normal. Just when he thought he was reaching her, she retreated like a cautious battlefield veteran. For every step forward, two steps backward were gained.

The intense, continual ache in his gut was for her—only for her. Tonight, he would have to be content with only the beauty of her mouth, ignoring the need to feel himself a part of her flesh, buried deep in the rapture of her body. Once again he would disregard the desire he felt tearing at him like a chain tight around his throat. For right now, the restraint was manageable.

What, he wondered, would happen when the bond was broken?

There was silence on the drive back to her house. A deep, hard silence that held each back from speaking until Rory pulled into Cat's driveway.

"You can't ignore what happened, Cat. I won't let

you.'' He killed the engine and removed his seat belt, shifting his body so that he faced her.

Cat sat immobile for a second before she undid her belt. ''You don't have much choice,'' she said.

''We both do. We need to discuss that kiss.''

''No we don't,'' she reiterated. That was the *last* thing she needed to do tonight. What she needed was to get inside the security of her home, away from him so that she could think clearly, rationally. Sitting here, in the warmth of the car, their breaths misting the windows, was hardly a good idea.

''Afraid to admit that you actually enjoyed it?''

Cat sliced him a withering glance.

He smiled. ''I thought so. Well,'' he said, pausing to lean closer to her, ''get used to it.''

''So sure of yourself, aren't you?'' she asked.

''Perhaps I'm surer of you.''

Exasperated, Cat opened her door.

Before she could get all the way out, Rory reached out and secured her arm. ''Tomorrow?''

''Can't.''

''Won't?''

''I'm going to my parents' for brunch. Alone.''

''Which means that I'm not invited.''

Was that a shade of disappointment she heard in his voice? ''It's a family thing.''

''I'm family. Or I will be in a few weeks.''

''But you're not *yet*,'' she stressed. ''Our marriage will be enough of a shock to them—hell, it's still a shock to me—so I'd rather prepare them.''

''They'll get used to it. So,'' he added softly, ''will you.''

''Getting used to something and actually enjoying it are two different things.''

"Is that a challenge?"

"No. Just a statement of fact."

"Facts can be altered to suit circumstances. Remember that."

"Are you sure you don't mean feelings?" she inquired as she stepped out of the car, shutting the door firmly behind her.

Rory chuckled to himself as he maneuvered his car back onto the main highway after watching to see that she got into her house without any difficulty. Her feelings about him would change. That was a fact he was determined to alter, come hell or Saint Patrick.

"Wow, is that the ring?" Lindsey exclaimed. "That's so cool. My mom thinks hers is the best. Wait'll she gets a look at this. She'll be green." Lindsey giggled at her remark. "Kinda appropriate, eh?"

Cat stared down at the stone, appreciating the small joke. The ring was beautiful, no doubt about that. "She just may be at that," Cat agreed. "Now, we'd best get you home."

"I can call my dad if you want."

"Would you?" Cat asked. "I don't want to leave Tara here alone, even if it's for a few minutes." She'd meant to ask Rory to give the girl a lift home, but their discussion had pushed it far from her mind.

"Sure." The teen shrugged, pulling her own cell phone from her jeans pocket and dialing her home.

About ten minutes later, Cat waved goodbye to Lindsey and locked the door behind her, turning off the downstairs lights. She stood there, one foot on the riser to the stairs, lost in thought.

About Rory.

About the ring.

About the kiss.

Her hand drifted to her mouth. Every other man's kisses in her life had been vanilla. Rory's were chocolate. Dark. Decadent. Rich. Like boardwalk fudge, once tasted, never forgotten, containing a secret ingredient that left you hankering for more. Another taste to compare. Another taste to roll around your tongue. Just one more....

It was something you never lost your appetite for. So you had to be careful, making sure to be moderate. Steadfast. Impervious to the little demon that urged you to "go for it." Particularly so if the voice had the faintest trace of an Irish accent, flavored by years spent there. Or wickedly blue Irish eyes that hadn't lost their ability to entice.

"Where's Tara?" Brian Kildare asked as he gathered together ingredients for his famous ham and three-cheese omelette.

"With her father," Cat replied, popping slices of bread and bagels into both the toaster and toaster oven.

"Oh," he said, one eyebrow rising considerably over his right eye. "So now he's her *father?*"

Cat lifted down a large plate from the overhead cabinet to hold the toast and bagels. "He was always that."

"Not so you'd notice," was the sharp retort as he whipped up the eggs to a frothy consistency and added the bite-sized ham chunks, then the combined cheeses shredded finely.

"Things will be different now."

"What's going to be different now?" asked a female voice.

Cat leaned over and gave her mother a kiss on the cheek as the older woman poured herself a cup of coffee.

"I would have brought you something, my darling," Cat's father said to his wife, "if I'd known you were up already. I wanted to let you sleep as you were in late last night."

"Thanks for the offer," Mary said, "but that wasn't necessary. Now," she added with a wicked gleam in her green eyes, "if we'd have been here alone, then that would have been wonderful."

"Ah, woman," Brian stated, "you're still a temptation to be reckoned with."

Mary placed a hand on her husband's chest. "And you wouldn't have it any other way, would you?"

Her dad lifted that hand and kissed the palm. "Certainly not."

Cat watched the play between her parents. Even after all their years together, there was still a flirtatious thread to their conversation, in the way they looked at one another, in the gentle touch of hands on skin. This was the kind of marriage that she wanted. The kind she'd grown up with.

Sympatico. That was the word. Brian and Mary Kildare had that in spades. An uncanny feel, each for the other, completely in tune.

"You said something was going to be different?" Mary asked, concentrating on her daughter now. "What did you mean by that, sweetheart?"

"Only that things have changed."

"How so?" Mary inquired as she pulled a pitcher of orange juice from the refrigerator. "What things?"

"I'd like to wait to answer that."

"For what?" Brian Kildare demanded.

"Until everyone's here."

"You've an announcement?"

Cat nodded in response to her mother's question. "Of sorts."

"And you won't give us a hint?"

"No, Mom, I can't. Not yet."

"All right then," Mary Kildare said, buttering some slices of toast. "We'll just have to wait until you're ready."

Cat read the speculative look in her mother's eyes, realizing that her mother probably had already guessed. She gave the older woman a slight nod of her head while her father tested the omelette pan to make sure it was the right temperature for his signature dish.

Moments later the front door was opened and a hearty baritone voice sounded a hello.

"In the kitchen, Brendan," Mary called out.

Cat's brother sauntered into the room, followed closely by his sister Kelly.

After the prerequisite round of kisses and hugs, coffee in hand, the family assembled around the long dining-room table. The sideboard held a variety of things for breakfast, some in warming pans.

"Where's my niece?" Brendan asked as he helped himself to a tall glass of chilled orange juice.

Cat, selecting one of the omelettes, paused. "With Rory."

Brendan's hazel eyes narrowed as he looked into his sister's face. "Have you lost your mind?"

"Thanks so much for that vote of confidence," she replied, adding a slice of wheat toast to her plate.

"Well, trusting him with Tara is certainly foolish."

"Because?" Cat demanded as she took her seat.

"Do I really need to enumerate reasons?"

"He won't hurt her."

Brendan took a seat opposite her. "That's more than I can say he did for her mother."

"Get used to Rory, Brendan. He'll be spending a lot more time with her in the future."

"Why?"

Cat reached into the pocket of her oatmeal-colored slacks and pulled out a small object. With an economical movement, she slipped it onto her finger and extended her hand. "Because of this."

"You're engaged?" her brother demanded.

"Formally, as of last night."

Brendan slammed one hand onto the table, shaking the cups and glasses.

"That's enough of that," his mother stated firmly.

"Sorry," Brendan said, quickly apologizing for his outburst. "It's just that I can't believe Cat is even considering such a decision."

"Nor can I," her father put in, giving his oldest daughter an incredulous look.

"But it is *my* decision," Cat stressed. "And I've made it."

"I for one am happy for you," Kelly stated, reaching over and hugging Cat from her seat next to her, then admiring the ring, an emerald oval center stone set in platinum, surrounded by two rows of smaller stones circling it. "He's got excellent taste."

"Yes, it's a lovely piece, isn't it?" Cat said.

"I wasn't talking about the ring, Cat," her sister corrected. "I meant you."

Cat gave her sister a smile of gratitude. "Thanks, Kelly."

"You really mean to go through with this marriage?" Brendan asked.

"I said yes."

"Then you can change your mind," he told her. "Hell, you wouldn't be the first woman to do that. Nor the last."

"I have no intention of changing my mind or going back on my word," Cat stated emphatically. "I said yes and meant it."

"Then," Mary said, leaving her seat at one end of the table and enfolding her daughter in a hug, "we're all happy for you."

"Speak for yourself, Mother," Brendan muttered darkly.

"It's your sister's life to live, no matter what you think, Brendan," his mother insisted as she resumed her chair. "She's made her choice."

"Or in this case, her bed," he retorted. "And she'll have to lie in it, with him."

"Brendan, please," Cat said. "You don't hear me bemoaning your lack of judgment in living with Celia, do you? How you could stand that cold excuse is beyond me."

Her brother stared at her across the width of the table. "You never said anything."

"Because when you were first together, she seemed to make you happy. That hasn't been the case in a long time, though, from what I've observed."

Brendan fell silent, his right hand resting against his mouth. "Doesn't matter, really. She and I aren't together anymore."

Cat could barely suppress the happiness in her voice. "You've dumped her?"

"It was a mutual decision. We agreed that we weren't really suited to one another."

Abruptly, Cat was all concern for her older brother. "And you're okay with that?"

"Sure." Brendan shrugged his shoulders. "Worked out for the best, actually. Besides, I need all my focus now for this upcoming trial. But my love life, or lack thereof, isn't what's important. It's you. And Tara."

"She's very happy with the prospect of my marrying Rory."

"Because she doesn't know him."

"She knows enough," Cat said.

"Does she know he's her biological father?"

"Not yet. I asked Rory to let me tell her after we were married."

"Why isn't he here with you?" her dad asked. "Can't face your family?"

"He wanted to come. I asked him not to."

"Why?"

"Because I had a good idea of how you'd all react."

Brian Kildare frowned. "What's that supposed to mean, my girl?"

"That she didn't want to start off her engagement with a battle royal between her family and her intended," Mary put in. "Can't say's I blame her."

'We're looking out for her," Brendan stated.

"Your sister can do that quite well by herself," Mary said. "She's been raised to."

Cat smiled in her mother's direction. "Thanks, Mom."

"No problem, darling."

Cat addressed her father and brother. "It's not that I don't appreciate your concern. I do. Really. However, it's not needed. I know what I'm doing."

Brian shot a look in his wife's direction, then in Cat's. "If you've set your mind to it, my girl, and there's no talking you out of it, then I wish you and him all the best."

"That didn't hurt, did it?" Mary teased.

For an answer, both Brian and Brendan Kildare dug their forks into their breakfasts.

"Have you set a date?" Kelly asked. Only she had been privy to her sister's apprehensions regarding a marriage to Rory, but she respected her sister's confidence and wouldn't say so to the rest of her family.

"In a few weeks."

"What?" her father bellowed, a fork filled with omelette halfway to his mouth.

"We thought it best for Tara's sake."

"Darling," her mother began, "there's a lot to do to plan a proper wedding."

Cat responded, "Rory is seeing to the details."

"And you're fine with that?"

"I've enough to do with the bookstore. We're in our busy period right now, what with Christmas less than two months away. His offer to see to it all was a blessing."

"If you say so," her mother replied. "What about your dress? Is he taking care of that too?"

"No. I want you and Kelly to come with me when we can all coordinate our schedules so that you both can help me pick out something to wear."

"I've love to," Mary said.

"Me too," Kelly added. "And I know the place you've got to try."

"Where's that?"

"In Philly. Just off Chestnut Street. This woman's stuff is to die for. She did Pam's dress," Kelly said, referring to her partner's wedding gown.

"Oh, that was lovely," Cat stated, remembering the simple yet elegant design of the dress. She'd admired it at the time. "Let's give her a try then."

"I'll get the phone number of her store from Pam, and we can take the train in. Have a regular girls' day out."

"Thanks. That would be great," Cat replied, and then finished eating her breakfast.

"Was I the only one who noticed that you didn't say you loved him?" her mother asked when they had a moment alone, about an hour later. Her brother and sister had left, along with Brian Kildare, who had been called back to work.

"If so, I appreciate your not saying anything then. That's all I would have needed."

"And do you love him?" her mother posed.

Cat wet her lips. "Not the same way I did before."

"Good."

Cat tilted her head. "Why good?"

"Because both of you were young and headstrong back then. Now you're both older. And wiser, I hope. As your love should be. Did you know that I turned down your father the first time he asked me?"

Cat was stunned. "No."

"Well, I did."

"Why?"

"I wasn't ready. Neither was your father. Though," Mary said with a smile, "he thought he was because we were sleeping together."

"You were?"

Mary laughed softly at her daughter's tone of voice. "Darling, don't sound so shocked. Your generation didn't discover sex. It was around quite a bit before."

Cat was still digesting this bit of history her mother had casually released when Mary spoke again. "I needed to focus on getting through medical school, and Brian wanted to be a detective. We both had goals to achieve separately before we could even think of handling them together.

"And," Mary added, "I wanted it to be forever. I had to be sure."

'Did you..." She couldn't ask her mother point-blank if she'd slept with someone other than her father. "*See* other men?" she finished.

Mary wasn't fooled by her daughter's question. "Did I *sleep* with anyone else, right?" She chuckled softly. "No. Not that I didn't have the opportunity, if I'd wanted to do so. There were interns and doctors aplenty to choose from, if that's all I wanted from a man. But I loved Brian. Knew it for certain whenever another man kissed me. Some were very good. Okay, one or two were wonderful kissers," she admitted wistfully, "but there was always something missing.

"After my dinner and movie date with the last interim man, I went right to your father's station house, since I knew he was working the late shift. Surprised him right then and there by kissing him in front of the duty sergeant's desk and asking him if that offer of marriage was still available."

Cat laughed.

"We got quite a round of applause, too."

"I can imagine you did."

"A month later we were married," Mary said. "At the right time for both of us. We might not have made it if we'd rushed in before. Do you see what I mean about me being glad that you and Rory waited until your love matured?"

Cat didn't have the heart to tell her mother the truth, so she simply nodded her head in agreement.

"So, if you've got some extra time this morning, why

don't we go to the bookstore and look at some bridal magazines for inspiration?''

Cat smiled. ''Sounds like a plan.''

''Good. Then I'll get my pager, and we can be off.''

Chapter Eleven

"Are you sure you're going to eat all of that?" Rory asked as a plate loaded with three buttermilk pancakes arrived for Tara.

The little girl nodded. "Just watch me," she challenged, pouring the warm syrup over the stack and adding a gob of butter.

Rory sat fascinated by his daughter's appetite, watching as she made her way through the first bite. "See," she said with a touch of smugness mixed with accomplishment, "I told you so."

He laughed. "That you did, my lady fair."

"Yours is gonna get cold," Tara scolded, taking another bite of hers.

"You're right," he replied, lifting a forkful of omelette to his mouth. Right about now Cat should be eating her breakfast, sharing it with her family, along with the news that they were to be wed. He wondered how that was going and wished that he was there, to lend whatever support she would need.

He'd called her early this morning to ask if he could see Tara while she was at her parents' house and was surprised when she readily agreed. For Tara it was a grand adventure, a chance to eat at the local Cedar Hill diner; for him, it was a chance to bond with his daughter, something that was becoming more and more important to him. After all, if he was going to be her real father soon, then he'd better get used to the idea, and so should she. Besides, for a man who never considered himself father material, Tara was stealing her very own corner of his heart, much to his surprise.

Now, if only wooing her mother was going as well.

"Oh look," Tara exclaimed. "There's Mrs. Hunter."

"And she is?" Rory asked, spying the cool, elegant blond woman coming toward their booth.

"My friend Lisa's mom. And do you know what they have at their house? They got lots of new puppies," she said wistfully.

"Puppies, eh?"

"Yeah." Her face brightened. "Golden retrievers, which are the bestest."

"Bestest?"

Tara bowed her head. "Best," she corrected.

"That's better."

"Hello, Tara," Mrs. Hunter said, pointedly eyeing the man who sat next to the little girl.

"Hi, Mrs. Hunter. Where's Lisa?"

"At home, still asleep, I'm afraid. She had a touch of a stomachache last night, and I came here to pick up some of their wonderful chicken and rice soup for her. It's Lisa's favorite."

Rory slid out of the booth and stood up, extending his

hand to the woman, observing the subtle shift of her eyes as she flicked them from his daughter's face to his. "I'm Rory Sullivan."

"He's gonna marry my mommy," Tara announced as the adults shook hands.

"Really?" Mrs. Hunter said, her voice filled with questions that she was too polite to ask.

"That's correct," he confirmed, sliding back into his seat.

"That is a surprise."

"To a lot of people, I'm sure it appears that way," he said, "but for us, it was inevitable."

Her glance flicked to Tara. "I'll say."

"Do you still have the puppies?" Tara asked, her eyes hopeful of an affirmative response.

"There are only four left from the litter," Mrs. Hunter explained. "We found good homes for the other five."

"They were so cute when they were born," the little girl said. "All fluffy and golden."

"They're even cuter now," the woman stated with a wide smile. 'Why don't you come over and see them again?"

"I'd really, really like that."

"Your soups up, Mrs. Hunter," a fresh-faced waitress announced as she walked by, a large tray in her hands filled with breakfast orders.

"Thanks, Cindy. I'll be right there." The cool blonde turned her attention back to Tara. "Remember, you're welcome any time to come and look at the puppies, Tara. But you'd better make it soon as I expect to have homes for them all by the end of the week."

Rory observed Tara's crestfallen look as the woman walked away to pick up her order at the counter. "You want one, don't you?"

She nodded.

"Have you talked to your mother about getting one?"

"She says that we have to wait." Tara dug her fork in and ate another mouthful of pancakes. "I don't know for what though. But," she added, "they really are the best puppies. I already know the one that I want, if it wasn't gone."

"Then what say you and I go and get it?"

"Without asking Mommy?"

"Let it be our little secret."

Her childish enthusiasm was tempered with caution. "You don't think she'll be upset, do you?"

"Let me worry about that."

"Really?"

"Truly."

Satisfied that he would take care of her mother's reluctance, she asked, "When?"

"Do you know where the Hunters live?"

"Uh-huh," Tara answered excitedly. "Not far down this same road."

"Do you think you could find it for me?"

"I think so." Her eyes got huge. "Are you really gonna take me to get a puppy?"

"I said I would, and I shall."

The little girl smiled. "I like it that you're marrying my mommy."

"I'll let you in on a little secret, Tara, so do I. Now, finish your pancakes, and we'll take a ride to see those pups."

"Tara thought we'd better come right away and take a look at the puppies, Mrs. Hunter. Is this a good time?"

"Sure. Come right on in." She ushered them into the

large Colonial farmhouse. "They're on the porch, out back. Follow me."

Rory and Tara walked with her, taking the long hallway past the huge kitchen and out onto an enclosed porch, where they could hear the excited yelps of the puppies. Nearby, resting on her own thick bed was the mother retriever, keeping a watchful eye on her litter.

Tara went over and petted the female dog on the head, letting the animal smell, then lick her hand. "This is Goldie," she told Rory.

Rory approached the animal cautiously since he was a stranger, bending down so that the dog could sniff him too, tossing in a few soft Gaelic phrases.

"She's a beauty, Mrs. Hunter."

"Thanks. Golden Glow is a champion. Won best of breed at Westminster two years ago."

"And the puppies' father?'

She smiled. "Another champion."

He rose. "Then they must be worth something."

"They are."

Rory calculated that whatever the puppy was worth, he would pay. The look of sheer joy on his daughter's face was priceless.

"Pick out the one you want, Tara," he instructed.

Her face was aglow. "I know the one I want," she reiterated, heading over to the deep open cage that held the puppies. He followed her as she leaned over, holding out her hand to the wriggling pups.

One caught his attention. The runt of the litter, he judged. The little dog scampered over its siblings, trying to get to Tara, yelping a hello. The other dogs were more laid-back, as if they were the ones picking and choosing.

Tara scooped up the runt and laughed when the pup licked her face, tongue lolling, tail wagging excitedly.

Rory reached in and picked out another one which was friendly, but nowhere near its sibling in affection and offbeat charm.

"What do you think about this one?" he suggested, holding out the other dog so that they could switch.

Tara took the pup and held it close, but her eyes were still on the one that Rory held.

His daughter had made a choice.

"It's okay," she said, "but it's not the one I want."

"Are you sure? There are several others as well."

Her chin lifted and she put the other dog back in the pen. "I want this one," she said, holding out her arms for the puppy that had licked Rory's chin.

He handed the animal back to his daughter. "Why?"

"Because she's so small. And she has so much love."

A sweet pain tugged at his heart, endearing the child even more to him. She had compassion and warmth to spare, a true testament to how Cat had raised her.

"You know it's a big responsibility taking care of a pet, don't you?" Rory asked Tara. "You can't get it just to have for a few weeks, then forget about it." That's what his parents had always said when he requested a puppy. And, no matter how many times he promised that he would care for a dog, his parents never relented, finding one excuse upon another to postpone the event, until finally he stopped asking.

"I know," she said. "You have to feed them, see that they have water, and walk them."

"And are you willing to do that?"

"Uh-huh." She hugged the puppy closer. "I promise I won't abandon her 'cause I love her already and Mommy taught me that you don't leave what you love."

Rory cupped his daughter's head. "Your mother is

right, my lady fair. You stay and fight for what you love
and never give up.''

"Then she's mine now?'' Her blue eyes, his eyes,
were wide and filled with hope and love.

"I do believe we've made our choice, Mrs. Hunter.''

"I figured that, Mr. Sullivan.''

"Can we take the pup now?''

"Certainly.''

"Can I go and show Lisa my dog?'' Tara asked,
barely containing her delight.

"She's in her bedroom, but go right ahead. Take the
back stairs in the kitchen.''

Tara hugged the puppy close and took off for her
friend's room.

"She's such an adorable child,'' Mrs. Hunter observed. "Well-behaved and open.''

"Cat's done a wonderful job, I agree,'' Rory stated,
reaching into his jacket for his checkbook. "Now, what
do I owe you?''

"Put it away, Mr. Sullivan.''

"Whatever for?''

"Cat once did me an enormous favor, and this is a
small token of repayment.''

"You're sure?''

"Positive. Our daughters are friends, so let's leave it
at that.''

He didn't miss the reference to *our* daughters. It was
her way of acknowledging the truth she saw clearly written on his face and Tara's. He silently applauded her
tact. "If you insist.''

"I do.'' She stepped closer. "May I offer my sincere
congratulations. Cat's a lovely person, and I'm glad that
she and Tara won't be alone any longer.'' She laughed
lightly, using a current catchphrase, "Not that there's

anything wrong with that, but it's nice to have someone to lean on every once in a while. Makes life a little easier and a whole lot nicer.''

"Have you picked out a name for her yet?" Rory asked as he and Tara made their way back to Cat's house after stopping at a local pet store and loading up on puppy food, a basket, blanket, toys and other items for the newest member of the family.

"Sunshine, then I can call her Sunny for short."

It quite fit the dog's exuberant personality. "Perfect choice," he said.

"I think Mommy will love her too, don't you?"

Rory reached out his hand and stroked the dog's fur, then chucked the puppy under its chin. "Who could resist this face?"

"Not Mommy, I hope."

"You let me handle her."

"What do you mean?"

"Smooth things out with her."

"Okay."

He hoped that Cat wouldn't have a major problem with the pet, nor with his taking Tara to get it. By rights he should have consulted her first, but this was a situation he couldn't pass up. Maybe a first test of her resolve to let him be an active participant in his daughter's life.

He would find out soon enough as he pulled into her driveway.

Immediately the front door opened and Cat appeared.

Tara was out of the car and running to her mother's side. "Mommy, look what I got."

Over Tara's head, Cat threw Rory a pointed look.

"Don't you want to hold her?" Tara offered. "Her name's Sunshine, but I'm gonna call her Sunny."

Cat accepted the pup, who proceeded to make Cat fall instantly under her spell as the dog licked and yelped her joy at yet another new adult.

"You'll let me keep her, won't you?" Tara asked.

Cat hadn't the heart to rip the light from her child's eyes now that the pet option was a *fait accompli.* "Of course you can keep her, Tara. It's obvious she loves you very much and that you love her."

"I do, Mommy, and I've already promised to take real good care of her. We got lots of stuff for her, including this leash."

"Then I suggest you put that to good use and take her for a short walk, let her get used to the leash. But stay where I can see you."

"I will. Come on, Sunny," Tara prompted, putting the puppy on the ground. "Let's take a walk and I can show you some of your new home."

"Was this your idea?" she demanded of Rory as soon as Tara was out of earshot.

"Guilty as charged." He explained the casual encounter with Mrs. Hunter at the diner and Tara's appeal for a pet. "You're not upset, are you?"

"I should be," she said. By all rights she should have chewed him out and told him to mind his own business. But, Tara was his business.

"I know it was overstepping my boundaries, but I couldn't resist when I saw her face. How much joy she expressed at the thought of having the animal."

How could she be mad at that? Cat asked herself. He wanted to make Tara happy, and didn't she? Rory was becoming a parent, wanting his child to have her heart's desire. "Well, any late-night *walks,* you're going to have to take, you know, after you move in."

"Gladly."

"We'll see about that when Sunny demands to be let out after you've just gone to sleep." She cast a glance down at his sage-green corduroy slacks. "Or chews your clothes for fun."

"Relax, Cat. I think I can handle it."

"You'd better, Rory, for Tara's sake, if nothing else."

Switching topics, he asked the question that had been in the back of his mind all morning, "How did it go with your family?"

"Basically like I expected."

"Are you okay with that?"

She thought that he sounded genuinely concerned. "I'm fine."

Rory sensed that she was being evasive, yet he chose not to pursue it right then, focusing instead on another subject. "Then how do you think your brother would feel if I asked him to be my best man?"

Cat couldn't keep the surprise from her voice. "Are you joking?"

"No. I'm not really close to anyone here to ask."

"You can't think of anyone else?"

"There's no one."

"Then you may have a very big problem."

"I'll speak to him."

"Maybe you'd better let me," she insisted.

"No, Cat. It's better if your brother and I have it out now, before the wedding."

"I don't think that's such a good idea." Especially knowing how hostile her brother was toward him, not a good idea indeed.

"After I finish talking to Brendan, if he refuses, then I'll try and find someone else."

"Get your alternate in mind, then," Cat suggested. "I know Brendan. Your charm won't work on him."

"Be that as it may, I'll still try."

"Then don't say I didn't warn you."

"I'll keep that in mind. Give me his address and I'll call on him now."

"He may be at his office."

"So noted. I know where the courthouse is, should I have to go there." Rory let his eyes drift down and sweep over her figure, taking note of the wool sweater that clung to her body like a lover's caress. It was a good choice of colors for her: the rich blue, green and rose blending on an oatmeal background. With her hair hanging loose, Cat didn't look much older than some of his students.

And he wanted her, like a thirsty man wanted water, because without it he would die.

"Are you free Wednesday night?"

"I think so, why?"

He noticed that she didn't hesitate in answering him. "I'd like you to accompany me to a small faculty party so that I can introduce you to some of my colleagues."

She considered his invitation for a moment before answering, considering what she had to wear. "I'd like that."

"I'll call you then later with details."

"I'd appreciate that, especially if it's a formal party."

"Not black-tie, no. But definitely dress-up."

"Good. That's a help. Now if you'll excuse me, I'd better get Tara inside and get the puppy acclimated to this house."

''I'll get the things we bought for the dog from my car.''

Cat had to smile at the thought of Rory schlepping puppy stuff in his expensive car. It was oddly funny and touching at the same time.

''Are you sure you won't reconsider talking to Brendan?'' she asked as he carried the items into the house and came back out.

Rory shook his head.

''Then do what you want,'' she said, realizing that she couldn't persuade him otherwise. ''You will anyway. Just don't say I didn't warn you.''

Rory kept that in mind when he drove to Brendan's town house, in the opposite direction from his own. Was he being extremely foolish in thinking that he could persuade her brother to be a part of their wedding? Would this backfire and cause an even bigger rift?

It was a risk he had to take. For the future. Their future.

His memories of Cat's older brother were sharp. Especially because that's how he thought of Brendan Kildare. Razor sharp, with a tightly focused legal mind. And a strong, protective love for both his sisters. He'd liked her brother. Enjoyed his company the few times they'd been together.

When he looked back on his time with Cat, that had been the closest he'd felt to a family; he realized now just what he'd missed growing up.

He stopped when he saw the sign that read Cedar Woods. Turn left, then third house on the right, Cat had told him. He saw a vintage white Corvette parked outside. Luckily there was an empty space next to it and he pulled in.

A moment later he was pressing the doorbell on number 212.

The door swung open, with stern-faced Brendan Kildare standing there. "What the hell do you want?" he growled.

"To talk with you."

"The only thing I want to hear you say is that you're getting out of my sister's life."

"Sorry, but I have no intention of doing that."

Brendan's hazel eyes were hard, implacable. "Then we have nothing to discuss. Now, if you don't mind, get the hell off my doorstep before I call the cops and report a trespasser. I'm sure that I'll have a quick response, too."

Left unspoken was the fact that Brendan was an assistant district attorney and that his father was a captain in the police force.

Rory countered, "That would be quite foolish, and you don't strike me as being the foolish sort."

"Spare me the insincere flattery. That may work on my sister, but it doesn't cut it with me. As for striking you, that thought has crossed my mind."

Only honesty would have any chance of working now, Rory realized. "I love Cat."

Brendan looked skeptical. "Sure you do. That's why you ran out on her seven years ago and left her pregnant and alone. Because you—" he sneered the next word "—*loved* her. Pardon me for doubting the veracity of that fact."

"Then let me come in and explain."

"You mean, give your alibi? Your version of the truth?"

"If that's how you'd like to see it."

"Like has nothing to do with it. I'm only interested in the truth. It's what I do."

"Then what have you got to lose?" Rory proposed. "If I fail to convince you, I'll leave."

Brendan pushed back the cuff of his sweater, checking his watch. "I'll give you five minutes."

Rory stepped inside his future brother-in-law's home, making a quick note of the dining-room table piled high with papers and legal tomes. A laptop computer rested there also, along with a well-used yellow legal pad filled with writing.

No hospitality was offered and none was expected.

The steel edge in Brendan's voice was exposed. "How can you claim to love my sister when all you've ever done is hurt her? What kind of love is that, you selfish bastard?"

"If you think that I'm going to argue with you, you're wrong, Brendan," Rory admitted honestly. "I was selfish. Remarkably so. It's how I was raised. Mind you, that's not an excuse, just a statement of fact. My world did revolve around me, until I met your sister. Things changed then, only I couldn't recognize it at the time. That didn't occur until after I went to Ireland. That separation made me rethink my actions."

"And you suddenly had this epiphany?"

Rory's lips curved into a smile. "Not so recently. It came upon me gradually. A dawning realization that I'd been a bloody fool who let the thing he loved best slip from his fingers because of arrogance, of hubris if you will. It's one thing to come to that conclusion, and another to act upon it. I didn't know if she'd moved on with her life. I certainly didn't know about my daughter. When the opportunity presented itself to me to come back here, I grabbed at it like a drowning man does a life jacket.''

Brendan couldn't believe what he was hearing. Either this man was telling the truth, which he could hardly credit, or he was a consummate liar who deserved an Oscar for his performance. Years in his job had honed Brendan's bs detector so that he could target a suspect's innocence or guilt within minutes, sometimes even faster than that. Yet right at this minute, he didn't know what to make of this man.

"Look, Brendan, I can't change the past, much as I would like to,'' Rory stated. ''All the wasted time when Cat and I could have been together. It's history, like what I teach, what I write about. And the purpose of studying history is to make sense of what happened, to learn from it. Well, I've learned. So has Cat. Painful lessons at times.

"Second chances aren't always given in life as I've discovered. Sometimes you have to reach out and grab them. I'm doing that with Cat because I believe we can make a go of it this time, for ourselves and for Tara.''

"Have you told Cat that you love her?''

"No. And I won't. She's not ready to hear it right yet.''

"Then how the hell did you get her to agree to marry you?'' Hazel eyes met blue. Comprehension dawned. "You used Tara, didn't you?''

"Yes.''

At least he didn't have the gall to lie, Brendan thought. "Did you threaten Cat?"

"Not in the way you think," Rory explained. "I simply let her think something that wasn't true."

"Like getting into a custody fight? That's the only thing that could quell my sister. She'd never put Tara through that."

"Nor would I," Rory admitted.

"But Cat doesn't know that, does she?"

"Not in her head, no."

"Don't you think she deserves to?"

"Haven't you ever bent the rules to get what you want?"

"I try not to."

"That's not what I asked," Rory said bluntly. He repeated his question. "Have you ever bent them?"

"Maybe slightly but never broke them."

"That's all I'm doing. For my family. To give us a chance, one we might not have if I didn't."

"And suppose that after your marry, Cat wants out? What then?"

"Then I'll let her go."

"As simple as that?"

"I wouldn't hold her if she was unhappy, if she really wanted to leave. You can't hold that which doesn't want to be held. If you can't let it go, then you never loved it in the first place. Cat taught me that. She's willing to let a piece of Tara's heart go because she loves her. And," he added with a touch of wise sadness, "she let *me* go when I needed to.

"I'm only asking for a chance to show her what we can have if she'll love me again. If I didn't believe that we could be happy, I'd never go through with this, Brendan.''

"How do I know you're telling the truth?"

"You know I am," Rory stated, looking the other man straight in the eye and not flinching.

The expression on Brendan's face softened as he relied on his instinct, something that hadn't failed him in the past. "Damned if I don't believe you."

Rory smiled. "Then I've got something to ask you."

Chapter Twelve

"So, you're really going to marry him?" asked a surprised Mary Alice as she took a good look at her employer's engagement ring.

"Yes, and I'd like you to come."

"What made you accept his offer, if you don't mind my asking," her assistant inquired as she poured herself a refill of coffee. Since the store wouldn't be opening for another half hour, Mary Alice didn't mind taking a few minutes to chat, when normally she would have been checking stock or preparing customer orders. And, while she'd been surprised by Cat's announcement, it didn't come as a total shock.

"A lot of things," Cat responded, not wanting to get into details for fear that Mary Alice would see right through her reasons.

"Tara had a lot to do with it, didn't she?"

So much for intentions. "To some extent."

"Then good. It's easy to see that she's becoming fonder of Professor Sullivan. They stopped in for a moment yesterday, and she couldn't wait to tell me about her new puppy, and that he'd taken her to get it."

Cat threw her assistant a curious look as she entered a column of figures into her computer. "They were here yesterday?"

Mary Alice nodded.

"What for?"

"Dr. Sullivan wanted to pick up some stationery. In fact," the older woman revealed, "he bought several packs of the hand-stenciled notecards with the Irish motifs."

Cat sipped her coffee. "That's interesting."

"I thought so. He seemed so happy to be with his daughter. You could see that in his eyes. And when he talked about you, well..." Mary Alice paused dramatically. "You could see how smitten he is with you."

"Smitten?" Cat asked.

"Oh my, yes. His face was so animated when he mentioned your name. Easy to see that he's a man in love."

In love. Cat found Mary Alice's observation strange. Was her assistant being overly romantic, trying to impose love where it clearly wasn't present?

"And that's good. Tara will have parents who adore her and each other. About time," Mary Alice pointed out, "that you realized that you still love him."

But she didn't, Cat thought. She couldn't. That was behind her, in the past, where it belonged. Where it had to remain. To think otherwise would be disastrous for her emotional well-being. Her heart couldn't withstand another blow like she'd endured before. To fall in love with Rory again would be an act of lunacy.

"So when's the wedding to take place? Next year? The holidays?"

"I should know soon."

Mary Alice's face was perplexed. "What? We are talking about *your* wedding here, aren't we?"

"Rory's taking care of the date. He wanted it to be soon."

"Sounds like he can't wait to make you his wife." Mary Alice chuckled. "No commitment phobia there, thank goodness." She put down her mug and hugged Cat. "I'm so thrilled for you. Happy endings don't always happen in real life, and to someone who certainly deserves one, but it's good to see that they can. You know, sometimes love is better the second time around. Makes you more appreciative and more tenacious in holding on to it."

Those words came back to haunt Cat later that night as she sat curled up on the couch, the fire lit in the hearth, the cream-colored sweater throw tossed over her as she browsed through several bridal magazines, looking for inspiration while she drank a cup of hot breakfast tea. Most of the dresses had a sameness to them that bored her. They were often far too fussy, or far too outrageous. Even if this was a wedding of convenience, it was *her* wedding. She wanted something that reflected her style, her taste.

Something that made a statement. Now, just what that statement was eluded her for the moment.

Romantic?

Practical?

Casual?

Formal?

She picked up the last in the stack, *Today's Romantic Weddings,* flipping through the pages, when something caught her eye. The clothes were stunning, with each successive page getting more and more intriguing. She kept, however, coming back to one page in particular, staring intently at the scene pictured there. It was an autumn wedding, late afternoon, when the setting sun drenched the photo in shades of gold, gilding the people and the garden of fall flowers with a patina that suggested a Renaissance painting, or the later works of the pre-Raphaelites.

Wildly romantic. Blatantly sensual. Charged with eroticism. The look on the bride's and groom's faces told the story. They were in love and couldn't wait to be alone, to seal their spoken promises with the union of their physical selves.

A solitary tear rolled down Cat's cheek, which she brushed quickly aside. She envied them. Their happiness. Their trust. And most importantly, their love. Love that sheltered and protected; that lived up to its promises; that held fast no matter what the obstacles. Love that grew stronger with every passing year.

The kind of love that she wanted.

She was shaken from her thoughts by a sharp knock on the front door.

Cat glanced at her watch. It was just after 10:00 p.m. Cautiously, she rose from her comfortable seat and padded barefoot to the door, her slippers forgotten in her haste. Peering through the small peephole, she immediately recognized her visitor. Sliding back the chain, she turned the lock below and pulled open the door.

Rory stood there, one hand resting casually on the jamb, as if this nocturnal visit was nothing out of the ordinary; his other hand held a leather briefcase. "I had to see you."

"Couldn't this wait until morning?"

''No. I have something that I want to show you right now.''

Cat sighed, wondering about the wisdom of letting him in right now. She was feeling too vulnerable, and he was looking far too handsome. ''Okay.''

Rory followed her into the den, wondering how flannel could look so damned sexy. On her it did. Hanging on a rack, man-tailored pajamas looked lifeless and boring. On her body, they looked as if they belonged, as if made to enhance.

''What's so important that you couldn't wait?''

He opened his briefcase, taking a seat next to her on the couch, the light of the fireplace and the small table lamp lending an intimacy to the meeting. ''These.''

Rory handed her a small stack of notecards, which she recognized as coming from her store, the same ones obviously that Mary Alice said he'd purchased.

''Look inside.''

She did, reading the hand-written wedding invitation.

Caitlyn Kildare and Rory Sullivan request the presence of your company at the celebration of their marriage at Saint Michael's Chapel, Cedar Hill University.

The date and time were also included.

''Do you approve?''

Her eyes met his. ''How did you get this done so quickly?''

''The wife of someone I know has a calligraphy business, so she did me a favor.'' He smiled. ''I doubled her usual fee if she would put a rush to it.''

''They're lovely.''

"Then if you have a list, I'll see that they're sent out."

"A list?"

"Of who you want to invite."

"Oh, that."

Rory smiled again. "Yes, that."

"My family."

"And what about friends?"

Now it was Cat's turn to smile. "Most of my family are that too."

A spasm of envy gripped him so tightly that it actually hurt. He covered it up with a devil-may-care smile. "Besides them."

"Yes, there are a few people that I'd like to see there."

"Then e-mail or call me tomorrow with your complete list, and it'll be taken care of." His gaze fell to the pile of magazines and to the open one in particular. Bending, he reached down and picked it up, noting the turned-down edge of a page. "Very lovely," he murmured.

Cat couldn't tell if he was being pleasant, or if he really meant it. "You really think so?"

Rory resisted the urge to grin, wondering if it was fate's design that they shared a similar concept of their wedding. "I do. It's almost exactly how I saw our wedding."

The soft look in her eyes was more temptation than he could resist. The magazine slid to the floor as he leaned toward her, capturing her head in his hands, then drawing her forward to meet his mouth.

Heaven. Pure, sweet and wild. The taste of honey and citrus on her tongue. The scent of it in her hair.

He moved closer, his body covering hers. He felt her

hands on him, slowly at first, then pushing at his leather jacket. Without removing his mouth from hers, he helped her with his own hands, ripping at it as if possessed. His denim shirt followed seconds later.

The texture of the flannel she wore rubbed provocatively against his naked chest. Beneath the material, he could feel the points of her breasts. But the fabric was in his way; he needed to feel them in his palm, under his lips. See them again.

Unable to keep his raging need under control, he swiftly removed the obstacle. Greedily, Rory filled his hands with the bounty he sought.

Cat came unglued at the touch of his skillful hands on her skin, her senses shattering at the impact. Memories were one thing—this was so much more. This was connection, both physical and emotional. This was pleasure to the nth degree, heating her blood, scorching her soul.

She gasped at the intensity of the sensations she was feeling, wondering how she'd lived so long without them. Like a sleepwalker, she'd been drifting through a fog, caught up in the swirls of the past. But this was the here and now, beckoning her toward a clear path.

His mouth left hers, wandering slowly along her neck, nipping kisses down her throat, across her shoulders, until it found the treasure it sought.

She clasped his head to her breast, inhaling sharply at the contact of tongue to nipple. ''Yes,'' she murmured softly at first, then louder, ''Yes!''

''Do you want me to stop?'' Rory asked a moment later, his voice husky with desire, his blue eyes dark as midnight.

Stop? No. No. No! her mind screamed.

Her answer was to pull his head to hers, lips locking in another explosive kiss.

Combustible. That's what they were together. Heat coupled with heat, getting hotter with each passing second, with each caress. A bonfire, not of vanity but of passion.

With a deft movement, Rory switched places; Cat now lay atop him, her full breasts resting on his chest. She eased up several inches, looking down into his face, pleased with what she saw there.

Lowering her head, she grazed her mouth across his hair-roughened chest, her lips seeking the flat nipples on his leanly muscled body.

His gasp brought a delighted smile to her face. "You like that?" she whispered.

"You have to ask?" he said, voice rough.

Cat wet her lips with her tongue as his hands slid down her back, to the arch of her spine, pulling her closer to the heat of his legs. She lay cradled between them, flannel against denim, the proof of his passion hard against her.

They slid to the floor, rolling over each other, landing with a thump.

"Mommy?" came a young feminine voice from upstairs.

"Damn!" Rory cursed, the mood compromised. He could see that in Cat's eyes. Seconds before they'd been languid, whereas now they were widening in awareness of the situation.

Cat found her voice. "Go back to sleep, Tara."

"I heard a noise," the child replied from her position at the top of the stairs.

"It was nothing," her mother assured her, rolling away from the man who reluctantly let her go.

Her face was warm, flushed with color as she grabbed for her abandoned pajama top, fastening the buttons as quickly as she could over her sensitive skin. "Go back to bed, Tara," she repeated. "I'll be up in just a minute."

She turned to look at the man lying on her floor, his eyes intent on her. "You'd better go," she said to Rory.

"Are you sure about that?" he demanded, sitting up.

Cat looked at him, at the warm, bare skin of his chest, at the deep, intense blue of his eyes, at the wicked tilt of his mouth.

Sure? She might never be sure of anything else again, but she was about this. "Yes."

He heard the regret in her voice, along with something else—shame? Confusion?

"It's all right, Cat," he said softly.

"Is it?"

"Of course." He didn't want to go. The proverbial wild horses couldn't drag him, but she could. With her softly worded command, she could get him to do just about anything she wanted, even if it was against his interests, against his true desires.

He reached out his hand and cupped her jaw, his thumb rubbing along her cheekbone. "It isn't over, Cat. It'll never be over between us. Don't you know that by now? This is just a postponement. Like all the years we've been apart." He got up, extending his hand to help her up, then reached for his abandoned shirt, shrugging his arms into it as she handed him the leather jacket.

"Is that Rory, Mommy?"

Cat walked out to the hallway, glancing up the darkened stairs. "I thought I told you to go back to bed, young lady."

"But I heard someone." Tara peered down the stairs. "Is it him?"

Rory joined Cat. "Yes, my lady fair, it's me. Now, do what your mother says," he told the little girl. "You've school in the morning, don't you?"

"Uh-huh."

"Then it's off to bed with you."

"'Night, Mommy. 'Night, Rory."

"Good night, Tara."

"Sunny is here too," she called down, cuddling the retriever pup in her arms.

"Good night, Sunny," he added, smiling at the small bark he heard in response to the words.

They stood there for a moment until they heard their daughter's footsteps recede.

Cat commented, "She loves that puppy."

"So, have you forgiven me for getting it for her?"

Cat smiled.

"I thought that you might when you saw her face. She's like you in that respect. Her feelings are out in the open, worn on her face for all to see."

Cat hoped that that wasn't true, for her feelings were all scrambled, like corn kernels in a hot-air popper. It wouldn't do for Rory to easily read how much of an effect he had on her. That was power, power she wasn't ready to acknowledge, not to him, and perhaps not to herself either.

"Don't forget about that list," he reminded her, stepping back into the den to pick up his briefcase before he headed to the front door.

"I won't."

"Then until then," Rory said softly, leaning over and kissing her on the cheek. That brief contact jolted through him like the slash of a knife. Quick and clean.

Not deep enough to wound, but serious enough to notice. She was the woman he wanted to welcome each sunrise and sunset with; the one he wanted to share decades of memories with as they grew older. She'd shown him love, taught him the nuances, and he couldn't go back to the emptiness of a life without her. That would be asking too much, expecting the impossible.

Cat went back into the den to see to the fire after Rory left, stirring the embers, giving herself time to reflect. Her glance fell to the sofa, to the rumpled indents where their bodies had lain. Passion had run hot, obliterating, for her temporarily, decorum and self-control. Without Tara's unexpected appearance, they would have consummated their undeniable attraction; there was no doubt in her mind regarding that. Slaked that craving as hedonistically as possible, denying nothing.

She sat back down, her arms wrapped around her raised legs, chin resting on her knees. And where would she be then?

Having a child was a blessing and a hindrance, Rory discovered.

If Tara hadn't interrupted, Cat would be in his arms now and the overwhelming tension between them resolved. The magic rekindled; the love reborn. He was sure of it.

His town house felt cold, even though the heat was on, as he entered. It was Cat's warmth he knew that he wanted. Her warmth he knew he needed.

Rory climbed the stairs and entered his bedroom, flipped on a single light, checked his phone messages and glanced at the framed photograph, a copy of the one that he'd taken from Cat. Soon he wouldn't need the photo on his nightstand. He'd have the real thing, both of them. The privilege of introducing them to anyone and everyone as *his* family.

Rory Sullivan's wife.

Rory Sullivan's child.

"Did you see the way he looked at her. God, like he could eat her up with a spoon and not share."

"Yeah, I saw," another feminine voice answered the first. "Our studly professor's not inclined to notice anyone else when Miss Kildare's in the damned room. Hell, even if she isn't in the room. Did you think you'd ever see the day? The original Irish heartbreaker, shackled for a turn at domestic bliss. Geez," the woman sneered, "it's enough to make me want to gag."

The other woman offered a brittle laugh. "You didn't hit on him, did you?"

"Duh!" the other snapped. "Of course I did. Not like Ron would give a damn if I did, so I figured, hey, why not give Mr. Handsome a try. Turned me down flat."

"You're losing your touch, Mabel."

"No I'm not," the woman protested. "Our Professor Sullivan just happens to be a man of scruples." She gave a delicate shudder, as if the thought was too mind-boggling to contemplate. "Who knew? Hell, I told him that no one need ever know if we had a little afternoon delight, and you know what he said?"

"Well, don't keep me waiting," her companion urged.

"That he was—" she paused, trying to hold back a laugh until she could finish the sentence "—saving himself for his wife."

"Get out!"

"Do you think I'd make that up? I thought it was a joke and that he was playing hard to get. You know, some men like to have the upper hand, makes them feel important, as if they were doing the choosing. I reiterated that we could keep it our little secret, that it had been so long for me, that my husband didn't understand, blah, blah.''

"How the hell did you keep a straight face when you said that?"

Her chuckle was sharp, like harsh metal. "Practice, my dear Emily, practice."

"Obviously, Sullivan didn't fall for the lonely woman-in-need routine."

"No, damn it, he didn't. He told me that *he* would know we'd slept together." She rolled her eyes.

"So?"

"Yeah, that's what I said."

"And did you ask him what he meant by that?"

"Of course. He said that he couldn't dishonor his promise to his fiancée. Dishonor? I just about fell over laughing at that. I mean, what is *that* all about?"

"He must have gotten some strange notions in Ireland when he lived there."

"I'll say," Mabel agreed. "All I wanted was a sample, a couple of hours at most of easygoing sex. It's not like I was asking for a commitment to a long-term affair. That's not my style."

"He's being faithful. You've got to admit," Emily noted, "that's novel and a bit romantic."

"Oh please, Em. Don't make me gag with that saccharine notion."

"That doesn't mean it can't be true."

"Well, whatever." Mabel shrugged. "Guess we'd better go back out before someone notices that we've taken a long time to *powder* our noses."

Emily chuckled.

Mabel admired herself in the mirror. "He'll never know what he passed up."

"Look on the bright side, Mabel. Maybe he'll be in the mood in a few months after the thrill of the marriage has worn off."

"So much for your belief in romance."

"Oh, I believe in that," Emily asserted with a dry laugh. "I just didn't say that I thought it lasted forever, now, did I?"

Cat waited until the two women exited the bathroom to come out of the stall and wash her hands. Her ears were still buzzing from what she'd overheard. One of them overtly offering herself to Rory, and him turning her down.

The idea that he wasn't sleeping around pleased Cat enormously.

But, another thought nagged at her—that didn't mean that he would never betray her. Kelly had thought the same about her ex-fiancé. It all boiled down to trust, and Cat wasn't sure about that.

And what could make her sure? Sure that he wouldn't leave again. Sure that he wouldn't fall into temptation and tear her world, and her heart, apart for a second time.

Trust.

Was she any closer to that with him? Tara trusted him. Cat could read that in her daughter's eyes. She saw the implicit trust and the growing love on Tara's face whenever she was with Rory, or talked about him, which she did, more and more.

Cat entered the smaller anteroom and checked her hair and makeup in the ornate gilt mirror. Retouching her lipstick, Cat smiled, pleased with her look. The ring that Rory had given her sparkled on her finger, reflecting the lights from the mirror and the wall sconces that flanked it. She'd borrowed a dress from her mother, a vintage black velvet with a deep V neckline edged with white lace, capped sleeves and a dramatic slit in the knee-length skirt. They might lack the height the rest of the Kildare family possessed, but what they missed there, they more than made up for elsewhere.

"Oh, there you are, my dear," said an older female voice. "Your fiancé is looking for you."

Cat smiled at the woman, wife of the university president. "Thanks, Mrs. Rodgers."

"Happy to be of help." Her round face beamed. "You two make an absolutely splendid-looking couple." The older woman glanced at herself in the mirror before turning to Cat and touching her arm. "Such a romantic story, my dear. I can't tell you how it warms my heart to see young people reunited and their love reborn." She smiled broadly. "Restores one's faith in this often-cynical world of ours, you know."

"Thank you," Cat murmured as they exited the elaborate bathroom.

"No, thank *you,* my dear," Mrs. Rodgers commented as they walked into the grand ballroom of the president's residence at Cedar Hill University. The older woman waved her hand in the opposite direction, signaling to someone. "I even told Evan, my husband, that I wanted to renew our vows this year. It's our thirtieth wedding anniversary."

"Thirty years?" Cat said as she was joined by Rory, who slid his arm around her waist and pulled her to him.

"Can you believe that?" Rory added, bending his head so that his lips brushed Cat's hair in an intimate caress. "I hope that Cat and I will be as happy as you and Professor Rodgers seem to be."

"I'm sure you will be, my dear," she said. "After

all, look what you've got going for you. Love and the opportunity to appreciate another chance. Plus a beautiful daughter.'' At Cat's wide-eyed look of apprehension, the older woman gave her a reassuring smile. ''Wasn't hard to figure that out when I saw the three of you at the Harvest Festival. Your daughter is the spitting image of her father. And my daddy didn't raise no fool,'' she quipped.

''Ah, the band is starting up again. Don't let me keep you from enjoying the music and most importantly, each other.'' She drifted off, leaving Cat and Rory alone, but only for a moment. A pair of women approached them as they were about to take to the dance floor.

''Ah, the happy couple. We've come to add our congratulations.''

Rory stiffened; his hand, which was holding Cat's, tightened. ''Cat, this is Mabel Prentice and Emily Bascomb.''

The women from the bathroom. Cat tilted her head, giving each one a thorough, dismissing glance.

''If there's anything we can do for either of you, don't hesitate to let us know,'' Mabel purred, moving ever so slightly closer toward Rory, like a predator sighting a long-awaited meal.

Hypocrite, Cat said silently. ''Thanks for the—'' she paused for a moment, controlling the urge to back the woman into the nearest potted plant, preferably something sharp ''—generous offer,'' Cat said, ''but we've got things under control. Now, Rory,'' she said, deliberately turning away from the other women and lowering her voice so that it was intimate, meant to exclude, ''what about that dance you promised me, darling.''

''Ladies,'' Rory said as he whisked Cat onto the floor and into the rhythm of the slow dance.

"What was that about?" he asked.

"Putting some people in their place."

"Meaning?"

What did it mean? she wondered.

The answer came swiftly. She was protecting her own. Against all comers. Giving notice that Rory was "hands off." Spoken for. Promised. Taken. Hers.

"Long story and not worth repeating," she replied.

Rory read the look on her face and the tone of her voice. "Does it have to do with Mabel and her attempt at seduction?"

Cat stared up at him.

"Jealous?" he asked.

"Do I have reason to be?"

"That's not what I asked."

"Yes," she replied plainly.

Rory smiled, pleased by her honest response. Cat cared. If she didn't, then it wouldn't matter who was hitting on him. "How'd you know?"

"I overheard her and her friend in the bathroom discussing us. I couldn't believe her gall. To offer congratulations when all she wanted was you, for a few hours at best."

"I didn't accept."

Cat gave him a bright smile. "I know."

Rory whispered in her ear as they went right into the next dance, still holding each other close. "You're all the woman I want, or need," he admitted. "And that's the truth. You have to trust me when I say that, Cat."

Trust. There was that word again. "Do I?"

"If you expect us to have a future together, you do. The decision's up to you. What do *you* want?"

Chapter Thirteen

Cat wanted to get married.

And she was. Today. In a matter of hours. Married because *she* wanted to. Because she wanted to make it real between herself and Rory. Lasting. An honest union of two people who had a future, not just a past. A claiming of a man and a woman, one to and for the other.

Ever since the night of the party at the university, Cat had realized the truth, a truth that had been staring her in the face, knocking at her heart for more time than she cared to admit—that she was still in love with Rory Sullivan. That she'd finally forgiven the hurt, let go of the what ifs and maybes, and moved on, toward a new chapter in her life. In their lives.

There'd been no time to tell him. The right moment never appeared, so it was a secret she hugged to herself, kept close in her heart. After the ceremony, when they were alone. Then she'd reveal that the vows she was taking today were honest and true.

That he might not feel quite the same was a fact she'd had to face. It couldn't be helped. However, she knew the spark was still there. Dormant, ready to burst into flame. She could build on that. Build on the strength of her love. Forge a new bond with him, one stronger than before.

Especially for Tara. Tara who was thrilled at being included in the small wedding party. The last couple of days she'd been practicing her walk, pretending the wicker basket she carried held flower petals, scattering them here and there, having a grand time. To say that she loved the dress Cat picked out for her was an understatement. Her daughter was over the moon, insisting on trying it on several times a day.

All that remained was telling Tara the truth. Explaining to the little girl that Rory was her real father; that they'd once loved one another; and that it unfortunately hadn't been enough to withstand their individual dreams, their singular careers. Then.

Now it would be different. Had to be, for all their sakes.

A gentle knock sounded on Cat's half-opened bedroom door.

"Come in," she called out from the bathroom.

Kelly walked in. "A limo just pulled up."

"Rory said that he was sending one."

"Well," Kelly said, stepping into the doorway of her sister's bathroom, "it's a doozy. White and very stretch!"

"Big enough for all of us, right?"

"And then some," Kelly chuckled. She gave her sister a thorough glance. "How you holding up?"

Cat smiled. "Pretty well."

"No more than that?"

"Better, actually."

"Nervous?"

"A little." Cat held up her hand and glanced at her ring, the thumb of her left hand rubbing over the stone.

"You can still back out if you want to."

"I don't. I'm ready to go through with the ceremony. More than ready."

Kelly stepped closer to her sister. "You're still in love with him, aren't you?"

Cat walked past her into the bedroom, checking her bed for her stockings. "I don't think I ever stopped," she said, pulling the sheer hose on and hooking them into the fancy garter belt, trimmed with white lace and embroidered rosebuds, a gift from her sister for the something new. "I thought I had. Figured that I'd gotten over him, but I hadn't." She went to her bureau and picked up a pair of earrings, then fastened the gold studs into her ears, a loan from her mother for the something borrowed. "If I had, then I would have found someone else before now. But I didn't even care to look. Even the dates that Mom and Brendan fixed me up with went nowhere because there wasn't anyplace for them to go. I know why now—it was Rory or no one. He was the key."

"To unlocking your love."

"Exactly. And if he hadn't come back, then I might have wondered why there wasn't anyone for me to love as I knew I had and could." Cat reached for the blue garter from its box, sliding it onto her thigh. Something blue.

"Hurrah for second chances."

Cat touched her sister's arm. "You'll get yours, Kelly. I'm sure of it."

Kelly shrugged. "I'm not worried about it, Cat. Really. If and when it happens, then it does."

"And so will Brendan."

"Speaking of our older brother, what gives with him agreeing to be Rory's best man? You could have knocked me over with a feather duster when I heard that."

"I don't know."

"He didn't tell you?"

"No. Neither did Rory. When I asked each of them, the only response I got was that Brendan agreed to do it for me. To make me happy."

"Strange," Kelly replied. "I would have bet money that Brendan would have rather seen Rory behind bars than married to you."

Cat gave her sister a rueful glance. "Me too."

"Makes me wonder what the real scoop is."

"Same here."

"Think we'll ever find out?"

Cat smiled. "I'll get it out of one of them eventually."

"Oh, I almost forgot," Kelly said, "what with all the excitement regarding the wedding," she said, a broad smile curving her lips. "My partner and I got the job."

Cat was excited for her sister. "The Australia contract?"

"Uh-huh."

She hugged Kelly, her pride in her sibling's accomplishment shining in her eyes. "Congratulations."

"Thanks."

"When's this going to take place?"

"I leave for Melbourne in a few weeks. Preliminary

stuff, mostly. Meetings with the client and some of his other people.''

''That sounds exciting.''

''It is. I can't wait. It's been a dream of mine to visit there, and now I get to do it for business.''

''Will you be gone long?''

''Not at first. Since I'll be the primary on this job, I'll have to go back frequently and see to the details once we're ready to start. I want to make sure that it's everything we discussed. This is a very big deal for my business, and I don't want anything to go wrong.''

''Nothing will, I'm sure,'' Cat said, trying to ease Kelly's worries. ''You'll be able to see Aunt Pat and meet our stepcousins. Now that should be fun. Mom said that they're a great family. Into a lot of things. You never know, Kelly, this could lead to something extraordinary.''

''I'd be happy if it led to more exposure for the firm and recognition of the work we do. That'd be good enough for me.'' Kelly glanced at her sister's dress hanging on a padded hanger in the walk-in closet. ''That's so beautiful. Rory won't know what hit him when he sees you in it.''

''It is, isn't it?'' Cat padded over and stroked her hand across the fabric.

''It's like the designer had you in mind.''

''You think so?''

''Oh yes. It's perfect. It's so you.''

''You don't think it's a bit much?''

''Of course not.''

''Then you'd better help me into it and let's get this show on the road. Thank goodness that Mom is seeing to Tara or I might be a nervous wreck.''

Another knock sounded on the open door. Mary Kildare walked inside, a package in her hand. "This just came for you by messenger," she said, handing the parcel over to Cat. "It's from Rory."

Cat took the padded envelope and pulled the tab that ripped it open. Inside was a white velvet jeweler's box, O'Doyle's, Dublin, stamped on the lid in fancy black script. Cat flipped open the lid of the rectangular box and gasped when she looked inside.

"What is it?" both her mother and sister asked, their curiosity engaged.

Cat held out the gift so that they could see.

"Oh my," Mary said.

"Wow," Kelly murmured.

"Is there a note?" Mary asked.

"Yes," Cat replied, handing the box to her sister while she removed the card from inside the padded envelope.

In Rory's bold hand were written the words *Something old,* which Cat read aloud.

"It goes with your ring," Kelly said, admiring the quality of the craftsmanship of the brooch. "Will you wear it today?"

Cat lifted the piece from the satin-lined box, holding it up. She watched the play of light as it bounced off the surface of the emerald. It was a truly unique piece, which she guessed to be Elizabethan. Something old indeed.

"I'd love to know the history of this jewel," Kelly said. "With something like this, it's got to be fascinating, I'm sure."

"So would I," her mother chimed in, "but right now I'd better go back to Tara and finish getting her ready." She gave Cat a quick hug. "See you in a few minutes."

With Kelly's assistance, Cat got into her dress, and made a final check on her appearance. The woman who stared back at her from the mirror looked radiant and happy beyond measure, eager for the culmination of the day's event. Ready to begin this next chapter.

In her heart, Cat prayed that Rory was too.

"Have you got the rings?"

"In my pocket."

"Just checking," Rory said as he adjusted the cravat he wore.

"My sister hasn't seen them yet, has she?"

"I showed her the design."

"But she hasn't read the inscription in hers, has she?"

"No."

"I didn't think so."

Rory's left eyebrow raised slightly. "But you did?"

Brendan laughed. "You bet I did, Sullivan."

"And?"

"I approve of the verse. Browning was always a favorite of mine. *'The best is yet to be.'*"

"Then we have that in common."

"You mean besides my sister and her child?"

"Tara's mine, too." Rory gave his soon-to-be-brother-in-law an ironic smile.

"Are you planning on telling Cat today what you told me?"

"As soon as we're alone, and the time is right, yes."

"Good. And don't forget your promise to me, because if you do," Brendan said in a silky tone, "and Cat's hurt again, in any way, you'll have me to answer to."

The truce between the two men was tenuous and each realized that, determined to see the day through for Cat's sake. One wrong word, one misinterpreted incident, could unravel the threads of their treaty.

"I'd like to think that if I had a sister, I would have loved her the way you love Cat."

Brendan accepted the compliment. "I care about both my sisters."

"A given," Rory stated thoughtfully. "You're close to both of them, especially Cat. I understand." Rory looked the other man square in the eyes. "You protect your own, Kildare. That's commendable. Well, so do I. And today, that passes to me."

Brendan's smile was challenging. "I'm sure you'll understand if I don't turn my back and walk away without keeping tabs. At least for a while."

Rory laughed softly and held out his hand. "Fair."

Brendan glanced down momentarily and slowly clasped Rory's hand before returning his gaze to his sister's soon-to-be-husband. "Make her happy, Sullivan," he adjured the other man. "Do that and we'll get along fine."

"You're sure about this?"

"Dad, you're only about the gazillionth person to ask me that today."

"A slight exaggeration, I'm sure," Brian Kildare replied with a twinkle in his eye as he stood in Cat's bedroom. He stared at his eldest daughter, a proud smile on his still-handsome face. "You're the picture of perfection, you know."

"And you're prejudiced," she stated with a light laugh, checking out her makeup one last time.

"My, ain't that the truth," he acknowledged. "All of my kids are special, each in their own way."

"We've got you and Mom to thank for that."

"I'd walk through fire for each and every one of you, you know that, don't you?"

Cat came closer to her dad, reaching out her hands to take his, then she stepped forward and cuddled close to his protective embrace. "I know."

"Then know this, my girl. I want you to be happy. The kind of happy that I've been with your mom. Over and beyond I'm sure what my fair share was to be. God's blessed me with a wonderful family and a wife that I love more now than I did when we said our vows. That's what I want for you, Kelly, and Brendan. The best that life has to offer. Sure, it doesn't come without bumps and bruises, but love's what holds it together, what gives you strength to go on through the tough times.

"I know you loved him once. Do you love him enough to put your heart in his hands once again? To trust that he won't drain you dry and move on? Because if you don't, then call it off before it goes any further. There's no shame in changing your mind."

Cat kissed his cheek, wiping away the smear of her cinnamon-hued lipstick with her fingertip. "I love him, Daddy. Enough to trust in the future. Enough to imagine us being together years from now with our grandchildren. Does that answer your question?"

"I thought..."

"That I never wanted him back in my life? So did I, at first. Then, little by little, that changed because Rory had changed. And I did too. Before, I realized, wasn't our time. This is."

"No doubts?" he inquired.

"Not about how I feel."

"What about how he feels?"

"I can't speak for him, Dad."

"Don't you think you should know?"

Cat's mouth curved into a smile. "I know all I need to know right now. The rest I'll sort through later."

"Later could be too late."

Her voice was strong and confident. "It won't be."

"Caitlyn."

"Did you trust your feelings for Mom when she asked you to wait to get married?"

Her father's face reflected his surprise at Cat's question. "Mary told you?"

"Yes."

"I loved her. That wasn't going to change."

"The same for me."

"Okay. I yield."

"Ready to walk me down the aisle then?"

He took her arm in his. "Let's go, my girl."

He stood waiting for her approach, oblivious to the people that made up the guest list. His eyes were focused on the woman who waited to walk down the aisle. Damn, but she was exquisite torture to his soul. Sweet, raw anguish that robbed his breath and stole his heart. He ached for her, could feel the need rising inside him, desperate for the merging of their combined flesh. He recalled the times that he'd banked his ardor, suppressing the desire to dispense with the sedate rituals of courtship and explore once again the magic that could overwhelm and captivate, magic stronger than distance or pride, magic that he could never willingly part with.

But before Cat's procession could begin, she was preceded by Tara in her capacity as flower girl. Rory was pleased at his daughter's gracefulness as she took each step carefully, strewing dried rose petals before her. She looked like a fairy-tale princess with her gold velvet dress, matching ribbons threaded through her tumbled black curls.

He gave her a big smile and she blew him a smacking

kiss, much to the delight of the guests, before joining her grandmother in the front pew.

Next to walk toward the altar was Kelly Kildare, resplendent in wine red. Cat's sister was striking, a tall goddess who glided down the path, her movements sure and steady. She took her place, giving him a nod of approval.

A hush fell over the assembled crowd when the chords were struck by the pianist in the loft as Cat walked in on the arm of her father.

Rory's breath caught in his throat as he watched her walk toward him. In her hands, she carried a small bouquet of flowers, mostly roses in various shades, white, brandy, peach, gold and red, mixed with baby's breath. His gaze dropped assessingly from her head, her golden-auburn hair done in Gibson-girl fashion, with a few tendrils trailing along her neck, to the moss-green neck ribbon that matched the velvet half-jacket she wore over her dress.

And what a dress, he thought, perfect for her in every detail. Instead of a traditional gown, Cat wore one that matched her individuality in mood. Keeping to the autumnal theme with its rich colors, her dress, a cream-colored satin gown, with its flowing skirt, was decorated with touches of the season. Embroidered flowers graced the hem and trailed down one side. A wide sash of moss green emphasized her waist and the curve of her hips, the color carried to the flat velvet slippers she wore. She could have stepped out of the pages of a magazine from a hundred years ago in her Edwardian outfit. Or the canvas of a Sargent oil.

And she wore his gift. It was pinned in a spot he couldn't miss—between the generous curves of her breasts that the deeply plunging V neck revealed.

Damn! When could he slip off this mask of dispassion and reveal his true feelings for her? His grip on the guise was getting stale.

Soon, he promised himself.

Cat could hear the soft murmur of voices around her as she strode with more confidence than she felt down the aisle. From the corner of her eye she could admire the sea of flowers that decorated the chapel. Fall colors dominated, giving the place a warm inviting look. She ignored the trembling that crept over her, tightening her grip on the bouquet that she held in one hand.

"You're almost there, little girl," her father whispered.

That was true. She could see the path ahead, where the wedding party awaited her. Saw the familiar and loving faces of her sister and brother as they smiled a welcome. Recognized the person who stood in front of the altar as the Reverend Kathleen duPres, her own minister.

Then her gaze fell to Rory.

Cat blinked and looked away momentarily, seeking someone else, anyone else. She found beaming faces of relatives and friends, traces of tears visible on her mother's cheeks as their eyes met, and then the happy grin on her daughter's face from her seat next to Mary.

She threw Tara a calm smile in return, knowing that her daughter was the predominate reason for the ceremony, at least from Rory's point of view.

Then, as if to mock her silent pronouncement, her gaze collided with the man waiting for her. The man who would be her husband, her partner in life, the father of their child.

Her heart beat faster, and a warmth invaded her belly. He was breathtakingly handsome, as always, but even more so today. Part of her suddenly wanted to run, to flee this gathering as fast as she could, escape while she had the chance.

Another part was drawn to the sensual promise that lay in those blue eyes, that could be felt in his strong arms. The dream that had once held her in thrall, and would again, if she let it.

Rory exuded polished self-assurance. From the shiny thick black hair that crowned his head, to the broad shoulders that needed no extra padding, to the starched whiteness of his pleated shirt, the silver cravat that was half-visible behind the black brocade vest with its old watch fob, to the lean line of his trousers, to the gleam of black leather shoes, he was man. All man, with no demarcation between the physical and the philosophical.

Rory held out his slender, long-fingered hand to her, a dazzling smile on his lips.

Cat hesitated only a second before placing her hand in the warmth of his. It was strong, capable, pulling her to his side with a gentle force.

She stood next to him, her body close. Rory whispered for her ears alone, ''From this point, my love, there is no turning back.''

My love. Cat heard that marvelous phrase buzzing about her head as the words to the ceremony were spoken. If only she could trust that they were true.

And what if they were?

''With this ring I thee wed.'' He repeated the words and slipped the wide gold band onto her finger.

Cat glanced down at it. She was now his wife under the law. Sullivan's bride.

When a similar ring was placed in her hand, she froze for a brief moment. Rory's larger hand was there, waiting for her to slip the matching band on his finger. Last night when they'd done the quick rehearsal, she hadn't given his wearing a ring much thought, assuming that he was going along with the ceremony, and not that he was intending to wear one.

Obviously she was wrong, and glad to be so. She slid the bigger band onto his finger and repeated the words that bound her to him. Kildare's husband.

"You may now kiss the bride," the reverend told the groom.

Cat expected a short, perfunctory kiss to seal the bargain and satisfy the typical requirements.

What she got instead sent shivers along her flesh despite the warmth of the late Indian summer afternoon. It was a kiss hot and deep as Rory held her chin in his hand and proceeded to instruct her mouth to his demand. She wanted to passively accept, to keep her cool, but she found herself sliding her arms around his neck and pulling him closer, accepting the kiss. Emotions that lay close to the surface, damped down, threatened to erupt.

Rory pulled back first, fighting to keep his breath regular. Once more reminded how much he enjoyed the physical act of merging his mouth to a woman's; it was comforting, pleasurable. With Cat it was different. Would always be so. Theirs was a passionate linking that went beyond the boundaries of mere pleasure to the threshold of truest intimacy.

Her face was a mirror to his own. The soul-deep shock he felt was there, caught and reflected in her green eyes. An intoxication so sweet, so pure, he ached in the deepest reaches of his soul to possess it fully. "Caitlyn," he said in an agonized whisper.

"Rory," was her reply, spoken with the same heaviness of tone.

Flashbulbs popped, intruding on the moment.

"Later," he murmured.

That word held all the promise she needed.

The promise had been postponed for the reception, a lavish catered affair that spared no expense. Champagne flowed as freely as the laughter and good wishes to the couple. A nearby mansion that doubled as a corporate event center had been rented for the occasion, one that specialized in doing the bridal party proud.

Cat couldn't get over the thought that Rory had gone to so much trouble to make their marriage of convenience special. She met the wedding planner, who waxed enthusiastic about Rory's involvement. "That's a man to hold on to," the woman stated, her eyes lit by a warm spark of interest as she picked up a crystal flute of the imported bubbly.

"I intend to," Cat replied, taking a small sip of the champagne, her eyes searching for Rory. She found him, dancing with their daughter. She smiled at the picture they made, dark head to dark head as Rory held the little girl in his arms. Tara was delighted, laughing, and sharing a moment with her father.

God, she wondered, what if he'd never come back?

But he had. And she was grateful to whatever whim of fate had sent him into her life again.

"You've never looked lovelier, Cat."

She turned her head, smiled at her assistant. "Thanks, Mary Alice."

"I know you'll probably be leaving soon for your honeymoon, but I just wanted to let you know that this was so special. Thanks for including me."

Cat touched her friend's hand. "My pleasure."

Mary Alice laughed. "Speaking of that, where's he taking you?"

Cat's cheeks warmed. "I don't know."

"Really?"

"Uh-huh. He told Kelly so that she could pack a bag for me."

"How romantic. Being whisked away to an unknown destination by a man who knows how to throw a wedding that'll have people talking for months. And a man, if I might add, who looks as happy as you."

A half hour later Cat was standing in one of the mansion's bedrooms changing from her gown to a relaxed outfit to travel in. Kelly was helping her, a big grin on her face.

"You're not going to tell me, are you?" Cat asked as she switched shoes.

Kelly laughed. "Nope. You'll see soon enough."

"See if I do the same for you," Cat said, referring to the fact that Kelly had caught the bridal bouquet.

"You'll be a long time waiting," the younger woman stated.

Cat replied, "That's what I thought."

"That's different."

"Is it?"

"Yeah, like Brendan catching the garter. Oh, that was something." Kelly rolled her eyes as she zipped up the garment bag that held the wedding outfit. "Having the garter slipped up your leg by your brother."

"Think of the implications," Cat pointed out. "Both of my siblings are soon to find true love."

"I'm in no hurry," Kelly countered. "And neither's Brendan."

"I found out that doesn't mean a thing."

Kelly threw her sister a knowing look. "You had a head start, remember?"

"No, I had love," Cat said, gazing at her wedding band.

"And soon you'll have privacy and a husband to contend with."

Contend? That wasn't the word Cat would have used, but she supposed that it fit. She would have to contend with the powerful sexual tension that grew hotter with each look, each touch.

Postponing the inevitable wasn't going to work. She saw that in his eyes, felt it in her bones.

Tonight was all the later they needed.

Chapter Fourteen

She was nervous.

No doubt about that. More nervous than when she first made love with Rory some seven years ago. They hadn't talked much on the chauffeured drive down to the shore, each content to sip lazily at the chilled champagne that waited for them inside the luxury car, along with the carefully prepared and presented hors d'oeuvres.

Cat hadn't eaten much of her wedding supper, so she was happy to nibble on the tiny works of culinary art and veggies. Besides, it gave her something to occupy her mouth and hands while she darted sidelong glances at her husband.

Husband.

That had a nice sound to it. A solid, permanent sound.

What few words they'd exchanged on the ride down were small talk, comments about the ceremony, the guests, her dress, Tara. Everything but what she wanted to say, wanted to hear.

"What made you choose the shore?" For some reason she'd expected something grander in scale. New York. Paris. Hawaii. The Caribbean.

"Can't you guess?" he said, his voice a husky whisper in the dim interior of the back seat.

A flush of color stole into her cheeks. *Well, duh!* she thought. It all made sense now.

"I thought you'd figure it out if you tried hard enough."

"Are we going to the same house?"

"No," he replied. "That was destroyed by a fire two years ago."

"That's too bad."

"But sources tell me," Rory said, "that this place is even better. With a spectacular view and a private beach."

"My sister designed a beach house for a Philly TV anchor somewhere near here," she said as she glanced out the window and caught a glimpse of a sign that indicated the small seashore town of Ocean Splendor. "Funny thing was, he never even got to live in it. He was sent overseas about a month after the house was completed."

"Really?"

There was something in Rory's tone that sent a warning through her. "But you already know that, don't you?"

"Uh-huh," he replied with a smile.

"Is that where we're going?"

"Would you like that?"

Cat recalled the scope of the place from the original drawings Kelly had shown her, and then from the house itself when she accompanied her sister on a quick drive down here to check out some last-minute details.

She didn't answer his question; instead, she posed one of her own. "How did you know about this place?"

"I met Marty Stewart in Dublin earlier this year while he was doing background for a story he was working on about the recent Irish peace talks. Long story short, he mentioned the house, and I didn't think much about it then. I contacted him a few weeks ago and asked if he was interested in selling."

"You bought it?"

"Yes."

"Why?"

"Because I wanted to."

"Is that the only reason?"

Rory gave her a lazy, sexy smile. "There were a few other reasons."

"Such as?"

"Tara loves the beach. She told me she had a wonderful time when you and several of your family came down to the shore this past summer. Now she won't need a special occasion to come down. It's here for her, anytime. And," he said, reaching out his hand and stroking his index finger lightly down Cat's cheek, "I know how you loved the shore. The fact that your sister designed the house was a bonus."

The limo pulled off the main road and onto a private one. A few hundred yards down the driveway, the lights of a house shone like a welcoming beacon in the darkness.

"Looks like someone's already been here," Cat remarked as she got out of the car.

"I hired a few staff to come in and clean up, stock it, and make sure that it was ready for us."

She drew in a deep breath. The air was cooler here, with a fresh sea breeze off the ocean, the tang of salt wonderfully evocative of past times. Rory was right— she did love it here.

The chauffeur unloaded their bags and used the key Rory gave him, opening up the door and taking in the suitcases.

Rory held out his hand to his wife. "Shall we?"

Cat wet her lips, then placed her hand in his. Sparks like a shot from a live wire jumped up her arm at the contact with his skin.

When they got to the door, he paused.

"What?" she asked.

"Can't be forgetting such a grand tradition, now, can we?"

Cat looked at the open doorway. "You don't have to bother if you'd rather not," she said.

"Oh, but I do, Mrs. Sullivan," he said as he swept her up into his arms, carrying her inside.

Cat clung to him, the smell of his cologne, masculine to the max, intoxicating her senses. She enjoyed the feel of his lean, powerful arms as they lifted her through the hallway and into the living room. There, he carefully put her down, as if she were a precious treasure.

A wide stone fireplace dominated one wall, the bright flames warm and inviting. She smiled at the conversation she'd had with Kelly regarding the huge hearth. Each was a sucker for a fireplace, deeming it wonderfully romantic. This house, Cat knew, had another sensational one in the large master suite upstairs. An overlarge stuffed couch in a dark red patterned floral print, and two matching oversized chairs gave the room a sense of welcome, as if inviting anyone to come in and linger.

The thick pile carpet in a mixture of sand and grayish-brown cushioned the feet.

"Do you like it?"

"What's not to like?" she murmured, feasting her eyes on the room, on the enormous wall of glass that faced the beach. "I didn't realize that Stewart had decorated before he sold the house."

"He didn't."

"You did this?"

"Me and an interior designer," Rory answered with a smile. "I told him what I wanted, and he made it happen. You'll have to see the other rooms and tell me if you like them."

The chauffeur appeared in the doorway with a discreet cough. "Your luggage is upstairs, sir. Now, if there's nothing else."

Rory took out his wallet and handed the man a large tip.

"That's not necessary, sir."

"Nonsense. Keep it," he insisted. "You have your instructions as to our pickup?"

"Tuesday morning, sir."

"Fine. My wife and I will see you then."

"I wish you and Mrs. Sullivan the best in your new life together," the man said in a sincere tone, tipping his hat and leaving them alone.

"Let me show you the other rooms." Rory took her hand, leading her through a furnished guest bedroom, an office, complete with computer equipment, and a large kitchen. "There's a deck off the kitchen so that you can sit out there and have your morning coffee, or whatever you wish." He watched as she checked out the appliances.

"Now, it's time to see the upstairs."

She wet her lips. "All right." Cat followed Rory as he led the way up the stairs. He opened the door to a large room, obviously the master suite. The pine bed inside was enormous. King-size and inviting. Their suitcases stood side by side at the foot of the bed, waiting suggestively.

He opened a door and showed her the bathroom, with its two skylights, malachite green tile, that covered the oversized shower and rimmed the big Jacuzzi. Plants hung from the buttery cream walls. It was like stepping into a tropical forest, wonderfully primitive and appealing.

"There are three other bedrooms up here as well," he said, taking her hand and leading her down the hallway. The first room was obviously planned for a little girl, with its soft tones of peach and white. A white wicker daybed, loaded with pillows, dominated one wall.

"Tara will love it," Cat said, admiring the fanciful shell border that lined the room. A small bookcase was filled with classic hardbacks; on top of it sat a basket filled with exotic shells of all sizes and shapes.

When he was finished showing her the other rooms, they went back to the master suite. "I'll leave you alone to get changed," he offered, "if you'd like."

"I'm not ready to do that yet," she stated. "I'd like to get something to eat, if you don't mind."

"No, I don't," he replied. "In fact, I could well do with something too, though I don't want a lot."

She smiled. "How about a couple of omelettes?"

"But of course," he replied in a patently false French accent.

Cat laughed. "Then why don't you make yourself comfortable in the living room, and I'll do the cooking."

"All right. I'll open up a bottle of champagne."

Cat worked in the kitchen, trying to keep her mind focused on the task at hand and away from the rest of the evening. Tonight there was no child to break the mood, or hide behind when things got complicated, which she was sure they would. He'd said he would wait, but after the episode at her house, she wondered about that promise being kept. She was on her own, and scared. Wondering how to tell Rory how she felt. Should she be bold and come right out with it? Or laid-back, waiting till the perfect moment?

Play it by ear or wax deliberate?

As she put the finishing touches on her culinary delight, Cat still wasn't sure what to do, praying the answer to her predicament would come soon.

He was nervous.

A completely unknown emotion for Rory, he acknowledged with a wry grin as he paced the room. Shed were the formal clothes he'd worn to his wedding. In their place he was dressed in a more casual style: a black cashmere turtleneck sweater and a pair of faded, tight jeans. His hair was slightly mussed from the many times he'd threaded his hands through it.

He felt like a schoolboy. Anxious. His emotions boiling just under the surface of his skin, threatening to erupt at any moment. All he could see in his mind's eye was Cat. As she'd looked earlier today, her face soft and glowing in the chapel. As she'd looked the night of the faculty party, confident and compelling. As she'd looked right before Tara's disembodied voice had interrupted their intense kisses, languid and willing.

He wanted her that way again. Now. Here. Ready to surrender.

Perhaps *surrender* wasn't quite the word he wanted.

Ready to meet him, he amended, no holds barred, no quarter given. An out-and-out meeting of honest equals. A man and woman who had nothing to lose and everything to gain.

Did she feel the same? He thought he read something in her eyes today while they were exchanging vows. A relaxing of the wariness he'd seen before. A willingness to make this union work.

Or was he delusional?

Damned if he could figure her out.

"Rory."

He spun around at the sound of her voice, the breath catching in his throat, the blood pounding in his veins, the heat pooling in his groin. He was achingly hot and hard, and ready to make this marriage real. As real as the love he felt for her.

"Cat."

The sound of his voice sent a ripple of pleasure skittering over her body, warming every inch. "Supper's ready."

"So's the champagne," he said, walking toward her to take the plates from her hands and place them on the wide space of the pine coffee table.

Cat sat down on the couch, sinking into the plush cushions, kicking off her high heels as she curled her legs under her. She took the fluted glass from her husband's hand and brought it to her lips.

"Not yet," he said, taking one for himself. He eased onto the couch, facing her. "I want to make a toast."

She laughed softly. "We've certainly had plenty of them today."

"This is private. Between us." His blue eyes went a shade darker, bordering on navy. "To Cat and Rory."

She clinked her glass to his, following his example,

draining the contents just as he did. "Hmm. I could easily develop a taste for this stuff," she said.

Now it was his turn to laugh. "This *stuff* is some of the best, my dear."

"Expensive?"

"You could say that," he commented, pouring them another round. When he casually named the price, Cat gasped.

"For one bottle?"

Rory nodded, making a mental note to get a case if she liked it. He certainly liked the look that came into her eyes as she drank. Soft. Dreamy. Relaxed. He let his eyes drift over her body, from the top of her head to the long legs that crossed at the ankles. She was wearing a silky white blouse tucked into a gray wool skirt. A skirt with numerous buttons holding it together, keeping him from seeing all of her legs.

Damn, but she looked prim and proper. Like a banker. Or a bookseller. Anything but a bride. His bride.

He inched closer, removing the glass from her hand.

Their lips met, and all else faded away. Questions, fears, doubts and ghosts vanished, pushed far aside so that they could indulge in the white-hot intensity that rapidly overtook them.

Rory's hands made short work of Cat's hairdo, removing the pins that held it in place, threading his fingers through the tumbled mass.

Slowly, as if he was unwrapping an eagerly awaited present, he undid the buttons of her blouse, pushing it back, exposing her silk-covered breasts to his eyes.

"Beautiful," he murmured. And they were. Full, plump, their nipples poking provocatively against the fabric. His head bent and his tongue laved the area, making the points, if possible, even stiffer.

While his mouth was engaged there, his hands were busy. One held her close, afraid that if he let go, she would disappear like a puff of smoke. The other slid down her rib cage, toward the braided leather belt. He loosened it, then moved to the buttons of her skirt.

Rory lifted his head and gazed lower. She was perfection, her body curving and ripe. His right hand followed the path of the oh-so-sexy garter belt, slipping beneath the tab that held the nude stocking in place. Her flesh trembled as his lips made contact with the skin of her inner thigh just as he unsnapped the belt from the stocking. He peeled it down her leg, stroking it off with ease. The mate soon joined the other stocking, along with the garter.

Only her bra and French-cut briefs remained. And his clothes. Clothes that were quickly proving far too tight for comfort. For expression.

Rory moved, lifting himself away from her. Standing, he didn't have the patience to wait for her hands to remove his sweater and jeans. He rapidly peeled the items from his body, all the while keeping eye contact with Cat.

He was more than ready. Never had he wanted anything in his life the way he wanted this. Everything between them had led to this moment, this fundamental joining that would alter the balance of their lives.

It had to be everything they'd shared and more. No holding back, no delays or regrets. Passion indulged, love committed, totally from beginning to end. Only themselves as sanctuary and true-home for the other.

The go-ahead signal could be read in her eyes.

It was all he needed to act. Ripping the thick quilt from its resting place on a nearby pine chest, Rory tossed it to the floor in front of the fireplace, saving their skin from the rug and its unforgiving pile.

The rest of their clothes scattered in haste, Rory scooped Cat's prone figure from the couch, placing her gently on the makeshift bed.

Protection was forgotten in the eagerness of the moment. Swept away by desire's tides, neither thought about the consequences as they gave in to the potent power of their union.

"I love you." No long speech. Just a simple declarative sentence that went straight to his heart when he entered her body, driving powerfully into her tight warmth.

She came totally unglued at his deep penetration, gasping aloud her thoughts, her feelings in one simple message, "I love you." And she did. More than before.

Cat clung to him, her nails scoring his sweat-slicked back, moving to the timeless rhythm he set, riding the wave as far as it could go before crashing upon the rocks and screaming his name in triumph. He drove her over the edge and delivered her to heaven.

Rory yielded to the primitive forces within his body, straining with the need to claim this woman in the most elemental way possible. Finally, driven wild by her cries, he erupted, filling her with his seed.

He thought it would be perfect. Hell, he didn't know the half of it. Sensational beyond compare. Wild beyond reason. Love beyond measure.

Cat snuggled in Rory's embrace, her heart still racing from the encounter. *Home.* She felt as if she'd come back to where she was supposed to be, back to the love she'd never really let go of.

"Rory," she said softly.

"Yes?" His voice was husky, barely above a whisper.

The time for honesty was now. "I love you."

A smile crept over his mouth. "So you said, quite vocally as I recall."

She adjusted her body, leaning on one arm so that he could see her face. "No, it just wasn't something I said in the throes of passion. I meant it."

His dark eyes bored into hers. "You did?"

"There's no doubt. I wanted you to know that. If our marriage has any chance of surviving, I have to be honest with you," she explained. "If I didn't love you, I couldn't have said my vows with as much conviction, with as much truth." She reached out and brushed back a lock of his hair. "I know why you married me, and I can accept that, but I have to think we can build on that. Get back what we had and make it even better, stronger."

He kissed her, his mouth capturing hers in a dramatic gesture. "Now it's my time for confessions."

'What do you mean?"

"I gambled that you wouldn't call my bluff. That you'd go through with the ceremony."

"What bluff?"

"That I would try and take Tara away from you. I used that situation shamelessly because I thought it was the only way I could get you back into my life, and my bed."

Her heart felt lighter. "You wouldn't have sued me for custody?"

"No." It was the way he said that word that convinced her. "That's what I told Brendan. It was all a ruse because I love you. Have for some time."

"Let me get this straight. You used my love for our daughter to get me to marry you?" He nodded. "Then, you explained that to my brother?" Another nod.

"Hmm. You must have given some speech to convince Brendan that you were sincere."

"It was the truth, and I think he finally realized that."

Her brother was sharp, not much got by him. Rory's words must have been ultra sincere. And if so, then he did love her. Really and truly.

"Can you forgive me?" he asked. "I didn't do it to hurt you, Cat. It was just the only way I could think of to keep you in my life. I was desperate, and it was my last card to play."

"How long have you known?" she asked.

"Known what?"

"That you love me?"

Rory took a deep breath. "It was maybe a few months after I left you and went to Ireland. I was angry that you hadn't come with me. And hurt," he revealed. "All my life I'd got everything I'd ever wanted. Handed to me, or easily within my reach, there for the taking. You were different. You were willing to say goodbye, to sever our relationship. And at that time, I resented that. Not only how dare you? But, how could you?

"I was determined to put the entire experience out of my mind. Chalk it up to a mistake and move on with my life. But I'd find myself thinking about you at odd times, wondering what you were doing. Who you were with. Did you love them more than you'd loved me?"

He'd been jealous. A small smile curved Cat's lips. Maybe later she'd let him know there'd been no one, but for right now... "What made you decide to come back and look me up?"

"Several things. I saw your Web site one day."

Cat made a mental note to say thanks to her cousin Alex for the idea of putting up a site and to Lindsey Reynolds for designing it. "And?"

"Then a good friend of mine was killed by a bomb blast in the North."

"Oh God, Rory."

"Some fanatic decided to blow up a pub to make a statement. The only statement he, or she, made was that some hate still lingers. But it can't win, or defeat hope so long as you don't give into despair.

"Sean was there, as was I, for a conference, presenting a paper. The only reason that I wasn't at the pub that night was that I was having dinner with my English editor, who'd decided at the last minute to fly over and see me about a new project."

Rory paused and Cat could see the lingering pain in his eyes at the memories. Her heart was momentarily chilled. He could have died, and she wouldn't have had this second opportunity for love. Nor would her daughter.

She couldn't stop the tears that welled in her eyes.

"Don't cry, my love," he whispered. "It doesn't matter now." Rory gathered her in his arms and held her tightly. "It was then that I knew for sure that I couldn't pretend any longer that I didn't love you, or want you back. It was like fate giving me another chance. One I had to take, or be forever haunted by what ifs."

He paused again. "You haven't said yet whether you forgive me?"

"Let me show you that I do," Cat responded, maneuvering out of his hold, then shifting her body so that she straddled him. Her lips connected with his, her tongue making a gentle foray into his mouth. Then she sat up, moving slowly, creating a gentle friction as she glided back and forth, taking charge.

Rory's response was immediate, filling her, letting her set the pace. His hands reached up to cup her breasts, feathering his fingertips across the hills of her flesh, rubbing the nipples into tight buds. Soon he couldn't remain passive, moving urgently along with her, as they both drove wildly to fruition.

Rory woke up as light filled the living room. It was still early as he checked his watch. He rolled over, looking for his wife, who wasn't around. "Cat?"

"I'm making coffee," she called out from the kitchen. "Stay there, and I'll bring it in."

Rory relaxed, remembering the events of the night before. And not just the night before, he smiled. Well into the early morning. Making up for all the years past and lost. Joining and fulfilling their destiny. Becoming closer than they'd ever been. This time there were no careers, no agendas, no plans. Only them, and the need that consumed them, again and again.

He lay on his stomach as Cat walked in. She saw the marks of her nails on his broad shoulders and slender back. Like an animal staking her territory, she'd marked him as her own. A blush tinged her cheeks as she recalled the endless hours of pleasure they'd shared. Love that went beyond the physical. Love that touched the soul and the heart. Love that filled and completed her.

She set the tray on the same table that she'd cleared the cold omelettes from a few hours ago when they'd gotten up to get food before returning to their bridal quilt.

Rory glanced up and saw that Cat was wearing a sweatshirt and pants. "Where were you? On the beach?"

"Not yet," she said, peeling the shirt over her head, revealing her bare skin beneath. "I took a walk and bought us breakfast."

"We have whatever we need here," he commented, unable to keep his gaze from her breasts. "Or was something missing?"

Cat pushed the pants off her hips and let them pool on the floor before stepping out of them. Her panties followed. "You could say that," she explained, opening the box of doughnuts she'd gone out to purchase.

His eyes twinkled. In her hand she held a large cream-filled doughnut. "And what, pray tell, are you planning on doing with that?"

"Just you watch." She joined Rory, pushing him back onto his stomach. She squeezed the doughnut, laying a strip of the cream along his back, over the welts. Her tongue licked them clean. "Turn over."

Rory complied willingly. A dollop of what was left touched each of his nipples. She bent and circled the area with her tongue, then sucked them clean.

She moved downward, following the arrow of dark hair, using up what was left, to Rory's surprise and gratitude. For him, another fantasy come to life. Then, smiling, she licked her lips, murmuring, "Breakfast of champions."

"I really didn't want to come home," Cat said as she unlocked the door to her house, the limo driver having just left them off.

Rory's smile was pure devilment. "I know, darling. I felt the same way."

"Only seeing Tara could have brought me back," she confided, turning around and kissing her husband quickly. She grabbed his hand and pulled him inside. "Welcome home, Mr. Sullivan."

"That sounds wonderful, Mrs. Sullivan." He drew her close to his side, looking around the hallway. There, on the small entrance table, newly delivered, was a Waterford vase filled with fresh flowers and a silver-framed photo of the two of them on their wedding day with Tara.

"How did these get here?" Cat asked, admiring all three items.

"Simple," he explained. "I got your sister to see to their arrival."

"This is an Irish piece," Cat noted, running her fingertips over the smooth surface of the little table, marveling at its rich texture and color.

"Yes. It just came up at auction a few weeks ago and I alerted my contact to bid on it for me. Right now," he added with a smile, "Irish furniture is all the rage for those restoring the grand old estates over there and here. Do you like it?"

"Of course," she said, as if that were a forgone conclusion.

"Then it's a gift well served."

She turned to him. "You don't have to give me things, Rory. All I want is you and your love."

"You have both."

"Then I'm well satisfied."

"Allow me to indulge my desire to spoil you and our daughter."

She knew that he wouldn't take no for an answer. "Then please, in moderation."

He laughed. "As you wish, my dear."

"Why do I think you'll do just as you please?"

"Ah," he sighed, "you know me so well."

"Much better after these past few days," she countered. "As I know my own heart, I now know yours."

"That's easy," he murmured, touching her face, rubbing his thumb across her lower lip. "It belongs to you. It always has from the moment we met."

Cat went eagerly into his arms, her mouth fusing with his, a prelude to a more intimate pairing.

The doorbell rang, breaking the mood. Cat flushed, as if being caught in something illicit.

"Darling, we *are* married."

She playfully poked at his ribs. "I know. Just give me time to get used to it. Necking in my hallway's a new experience for me."

"You'll have to tell me later why that's so," he said, "but right now I think we should answer the door."

As soon as the door swung open, a chubby golden retriever pup sped into the house, yapping excitedly while Tara launched herself into her mother's waiting arms.

"I missed you, sweetheart," Cat said, hugging her daughter tightly and placing a kiss on her cheek.

Tara did likewise, then wiggled from her mom's grasp to dash to Rory, who lifted her high in the air and swirled her around. "Miss me too?"

"Lots and lots," the little girl said. "So did Sunny."

"Then why not take her upstairs, and we'll be up in just a minute, my lady fair. Your mother and I have something to tell you."

"If it's about you being my real daddy, I already know," she stated with a smile.

"What?" Both Cat and Rory asked. Cat turned her focus to her mother, standing in the doorway.

"Don't look at me," Mary protested. "I'm as shocked as you. And, much as I'd like to hear the details, *all* the details, I'm due to make rounds in twenty minutes, so I've got to leave." She kissed her daughter and new son-in-law. "Make my girls happy, Rory, and you'll get no grief from me. Bye.'' With that she left, leaving the family alone.

"How did you find that out?" Cat demanded softly.

Tara let out a dramatic sigh. "I'm not stupid, Mommy. All I had to do was look in the mirror, and I saw his face. Just because I'm six doesn't mean I'm dumb, you know."

"Of course it doesn't, my lady fair." Rory bent down and took hold of Tara's arms lightly. "You don't mind then?"

"It's kinda neat, I think," she said, head cocked to one side. "Like something magical and very special."

"No, you and your mom are the special ones," Rory insisted, gathering his daughter into his arms and his wife to his side. "You both brought light and magic into my life. Without the two of you I'd be a much poorer man."

"And you're gonna stay?" Tara asked.

He kissed the little girl's cheek. "Forever, if you'll let me."

"From this day forward," Cat quoted, "'The best is yet to be.'"

Epilogue

Thanksgiving had always been an important holiday for the Kildares. It was the one time they made to get together without fail. Mary insisted on that. No matter what, Thanksgiving dinner was a family event, meant to be shared.

This year another place was set at the table. Another person was welcomed into the festivities.

This, Cat thought as she helped her mother in the kitchen, mixing up a huge bowl of salad, was the true test of her family's acceptance of Rory. While there had been a few uneasy moments over the past month, this was the ultimate pass-or-fail exam.

"How do you think it's going?" asked Kelly, cutting up a large plate of vegetables for the dip.

Cat laughed. "Pretty good, I'd say. No sounds of bloodshed or mayhem from the living room."

"Could be a ruse to lure us into a false state of security."

"Or," Cat mused, "it could be that Dad and Brendan are finally accepting Rory." Cat eyed her sister. "You have, right?"

"He makes you happy and that's good enough for me," Kelly said. "He loves you and Tara. That's plain enough to see and easy to understand. Though that's not to say that if he hurt you again, he wouldn't be in big trouble." She put a carrot stick into the chopper, pressed a button, then watched it come out as shreds.

Cat chuckled, then switched subjects. "That's a nice tan you've got there," commenting on Kelly's golden skin.

"Would you believe that this is the result of two days in the Aussie sun?"

"That's right, it's springtime there, isn't it?"

"Which isn't to say that they can't have all four seasons in the space of twenty-four to forty-eight hours as I've discovered. But it's a beautiful land."

"And how are the men?"

"The men are men."

"Duh?" Cat asked, hands on her hips, a puzzled look on her face. "What's that supposed to mean?"

"I'd better take this in," Kelly said, ignoring her sister's question, adding a thick scoop of her homemade dip to the small bowl in the center of the glass tray.

As Kelly made her retreat, Brendan entered the kitchen, heading for the refrigerator. He leaned in and brought out three cold bottles of beer, flipped off the top of one of them with a handy bottle opener and drank, draining almost half the bottle.

"Thirsty?"

Brendan wiped away the traces of foam from his mouth with the back of his hand. "Somewhat."

Cat noticed the guarded answer. Her older brother was in his lawyer mode, playing it cool and close.

"I didn't ask if you thought the beer was guilty, just if you were thirsty."

"Sorry. What?" he asked.

"It's that case, isn't it?"

He leveled a direct glance at her. "You know I can't talk about it, Cat."

"I know. It's just that you look so tired that I'm worried about you."

"I'm all right," he insisted.

Her concern filtered through her voice. "You look like you've lost weight."

"Nonsense."

"Don't neglect your health, or your heart, for the job, Brendan."

"Well, who died and named you CEO?" His smile took the sting from his words.

"Just a worried sister."

"Don't worry about me," he chided. "I just beat your husband at chess."

"Are you sure he didn't let you win," she teased, "like I used to do?"

"You wish!"

Cat laughed. "Thanks for making the effort to include him, Brendan. It means a lot to me, and I know it does to Rory also."

"I said that I'd try, and I'm a man of my word, sis."

"That you are. And," she said, kissing his cheek, "the best brother a girl could have."

"You got that right. Now, I'd better take these beers out before Dad wonders what happened to me."

"I was just coming to check," Rory stated as he strolled into the room.

"Here's yours," Brendan said, handing Rory one of the tall, cold bottles, leaving them alone.

Rory slipped up behind Cat and wrapped his arms around her.

She leaned into his chest, savoring the moment, and the feel of his strong arms around her.

"Thank you," he whispered into her hair.

"For what?"

"For giving me what I wanted most—a family."

She turned in his arms, her hand lifting to stroke his cheek. "My pleasure." She debated about telling him her news there, wanting to share it in private, but somehow now seemed right. "Our family'll be expanding."

"You've got more relatives coming?"

She smiled, taking his hand and placing it on her stomach. "You do," she said. "A son or another daughter."

"Another child?"

She shook her head. "Uh-huh."

"Our honeymoon," he said, a wide smile curving his mouth. Rory bent his head and kissed her softly. "Our child." His hand spread over her belly, fingers splayed over the wool of her wine-colored jumper.

"God, how I love you."

She laid her head on his broad chest. "No more than I you."

"This time, together," he murmured.

"This time, forever," she replied.

* * * * *

Beloved author
JOAN ELLIOTT PICKART
reprises her successful miniseries
THE BABY BET
with the following delightful stories:

On sale June 2000
TO A MacALLISTER BORN
Silhouette Special Edition® #1329
The Bachelor Bet's Jennifer Mackane proves more than
a match for marriage-wary Jack MacAllister.

On Sale July 2000
THE BABY BET: HIS SECRET SON
Silhouette Books®
A secret son stirs up trouble for patriarch
Robert MacAllister and the clan.

On sale October 2000
BABY: MacALLISTER-MADE
Silhouette Desire® #1326
A night of passion has bachelor Richard MacAllister awaiting
the next bouncing MacAllister bundle!

And coming to Special Edition® in 2001:
HER LITTLE SECRET.

Available at your favorite retail outlet.

Where love comes alive™

Visit Silhouette at www.eHarlequin.com

SSEBET

If you enjoyed what you just read,
then we've got an offer you can't resist!

Take 2 bestselling love stories FREE!
Plus get a FREE surprise gift!

Want surprises? Adventure? Seduction? Secrets? Emotion?

All in one book?

You've got it!

In June 2000 Silhouette is proud to present:

SENSATIONAL

This special collection contains
four complete novels, one from each
of your favorite series, and features some
of your most beloved authors...

all for one low price!

Sharon Sala—Intimate Moments
Elizabeth Bevarly—Desire
Sandra Steffen—Romance
Cheryl Reavis—Special Edition

You won't be disappointed!

Available at your favorite retail outlet.

Silhouette®
Where love comes alive™

SILHOUETTE'S 20TH ANNIVERSARY CONTEST
OFFICIAL RULES
NO PURCHASE NECESSARY TO ENTER

1. To enter, follow directions published in the offer to which you are responding. Contest begins 1/1/00 and ends on 8/24/00 (the "Promotion Period"). Method of entry may vary. Mailed entries must be postmarked by 8/24/00, and received by 8/31/00.

2. During the Promotion Period, the Contest may be presented via the Internet. Entry via the Internet may be restricted to residents of certain geographic areas that are disclosed on the Web site. To enter via the Internet, if you are a resident of a geographic area in which Internet entry is permissible, follow the directions displayed on-line, including typing your essay of 100 words or fewer telling us "Where In The World Your Love Will Come Alive." On-line entries must be received by 11:59 p.m. Eastern Standard time on 8/24/00. Limit one e-mail entry per person, household and e-mail address per day, per presentation. If you are a resident of a geographic area in which entry via the Internet is permissible, you may, in lieu of submitting an entry on-line, enter by mail, by hand-printing your name, address, telephone number and contest number/name on an 8"x 11" plain piece of paper and telling us in 100 words or fewer "Where In The World Your Love Will Come Alive," and mailing via first-class mail to: Silhouette 20th Anniversary Contest, (in the U.S.) P.O. Box 9069, Buffalo, NY 14269-9069; (In Canada) P.O. Box 637, Fort Erie, Ontario, Canada L2A 5X3. Limit one 8"x 11" mailed entry per person, household and e-mail address per day. On-line and/or 8"x 11" mailed entries received from persons residing in geographic areas in which Internet entry is not permissible will be disqualified. No liability is assumed for lost, late, incomplete, inaccurate, nondelivered or misdirected mail, or misdirected e-mail, for technical, hardware or software failures of any kind, lost or unavailable network connection, or failed, incomplete, garbled or delayed computer transmission or any human error which may occur in the receipt or processing of the entries in the contest.

3. Essays will be judged by a panel of members of the Silhouette editorial and marketing staff based on the following criteria:

   Sincerity (believability, credibility)—50%

   Originality (freshness, creativity)—30%

   Aptness (appropriateness to contest ideas)—20%

   Purchase or acceptance of a product offer does not improve your chances of winning. In the event of a tie, duplicate prizes will be awarded.

4. All entries become the property of Harlequin Enterprises Ltd., and will not be returned. Winner will be determined no later than 10/31/00 and will be notified by mail. Grand Prize winner will be required to sign and return Affidavit of Eligibility within 15 days of receipt of notification. Noncompliance within the time period may result in disqualification and an alternative winner may be selected. All municipal, provincial, federal, state and local laws and regulations apply. Contest open only to residents of the U.S. and Canada who are 18 years of age or older, and is void wherever prohibited by law. Internet entry is restricted solely to residents of those geographical areas in which Internet entry is permissible. Employees of Torstar Corp., their affiliates, agents and members of their immediate families are not eligible. Taxes on the prizes are the sole responsibility of winners. Entry and acceptance of any prize offered constitutes permission to use winner's name, photograph or other likeness for the purposes of advertising, trade and promotion on behalf of Torstar Corp. without further compensation to the winner, unless prohibited by law. Torstar Corp and D.L. Blair, Inc., their parents, affiliates and subsidiaries, are not responsible for errors in printing or electronic presentation of contest or entries. In the event of printing or other errors which may result in unintended prize values or duplication of prizes, all affected contest materials or entries shall be null and void. If for any reason the Internet portion of the contest is not capable of running as planned, including infection by computer virus, bugs, tampering, unauthorized intervention, fraud, technical failures, or any other causes beyond the control of Torstar Corp. which corrupt or affect the administration, secrecy, fairness, integrity or proper conduct of the contest, Torstar Corp. reserves the right, at its sole discretion, to disqualify any individual who tampers with the entry process and to cancel, terminate, modify or suspend the contest or the Internet portion thereof. In the event of a dispute regarding an on-line entry, the entry will be deemed submitted by the authorized holder of the e-mail account submitted at the time of entry. Authorized account holder is defined as the natural person who is assigned to an e-mail address by an Internet access provider, on-line service provider or other organization that is responsible for arranging e-mail address for the domain associated with the submitted e-mail address.

5. Prizes: Grand Prize—a $10,000 vacation to anywhere in the world. Travelers (at least one must be 18 years of age or older) or parent or guardian if one traveler is a minor, must sign and return a Release of Liability prior to departure. Travel must be completed by December 31, 2001, and is subject to space and accommodations availability. Two hundred (200) Second Prizes—a two-book limited edition autographed collector set from one of the Silhouette Anniversary authors: Nora Roberts, Diana Palmer, Linda Howard or Annette Broadrick (value $10.00 each set). All prizes are valued in U.S. dollars.

6. For a list of winners (available after 10/31/00), send a self-addressed, stamped envelope to: Harlequin Silhouette 20th Anniversary Winners, P.O. Box 4200, Blair, NE 68009-4200.

Contest sponsored by Torstar Corp., P.O. Box 9042, Buffalo, NY 14269-9042.

PS20RULES